A MOON LAKE CHRONICLES MYSTERY

The Evil Within

Leah Brewer

ISBN-13: 9798509124389
ISBN-10: 1477123456

Cover design by: Art Painter
Library of Congress Control Number: 2018675309
Printed in the United States of America

For my husband, Mark
who has been my Henry since the day we met,
and my two daughters, Cassidy and Carissa,
who inspire me to try to do better every day,
and my son-in-law, Logan
who treats Cassidy like Geoffrey treats Rose.

CONTENTS

ABOUT

Chrissy Bennett has lost a lot in her life. Her parents. Her husband. Her life back home. Now yet another loss brings her and her two young daughters' home to Moon Lake. Home to The Kensington Lodge, where she spent most of her childhood.

Will the memories she finds there be what she is looking for? Or will she find a deadly mystery centered around her family that goes back for centuries?

Henry Kesselberg lives his life protecting humans but never getting close enough to a woman to feel real love. Running the agency gives him purpose and meaning in his life—something he desperately needs.

Things suddenly change after he is bound to fulfill a promise. A promise to look after his dearest friend's niece in the case of his friend's passing. He travels to Moon Lake to live up to that promise. Will the things he finds there help his tortured soul find love? Or will he also be caught up in a deadly mystery that could impact everything he has worked to overcome?

PROLOGUE

Near the Arkansas Post
August 1795

"Lucas, there's an opening down here!" Ronald Burgess yelled toward Lucas Rollings as he eased down and in between two massive rock formations.

"I still don't know about this, Ronald." Lucas Rollings answered nervously. "What if the legends are true?"

"That's ridiculous. Those so-called legends are stories told to scare people. You know, like made-up ghost stories."

"At least let me tell a few of the other men where we're going. I'd hate for us to get caught up in something and them not know where to look for us!"

"Better yet, why don't you see if you can find two or three men to come down here and help us explore. I'll head down to make sure we have a clear path."

Ronald was too impatient to wait on anyone, so he continued down the opening. Suddenly, he let out a yelp as he lost footing and slid down a large, flat boulder. He caught his breath when he landed just a few feet below and realized he didn't have any injuries.

The only source of light was the opening he had just come from, so he had to feel around to get an idea of his surroundings.

He didn't want to venture too far without light since he could hear water running.

"LUCAS! Where are you at?"

"Hold your horses! We're coming as fast as we can!"

"Well, hold up. Take the lamp and use it to watch your footing. It's slicker than snot on a doorknob coming down."

Ronald looked up and saw Lucas scooting down the boulder with Bradley Whitmore, George Watkins, Matthew Kensington, and Arthur Hamilton following closely behind him. Sure, they were making their way down a lot easier since he had done all the hard work for them.

"I was able to get a few men to help us explore." Lucas commented to Ronald.

They had walked almost ten minutes before the cave separated into two different paths.

"Alright, gentlemen, let's split up. That will make treasure hunting quicker if we have two different parties. Arthur, you go with Lucas and Bradley. George, you and Matt are with me." Ronald knew he was a natural-born leader, so no one should be surprised that he stepped up and gave instructions. Lucas led the two men with him to the left while Ronald and the rest of the group kept going on the current path.

Within a few more minutes, they heard a loud flowing sound. "What do y'all s'pose that is?" George posed the question that the other two were thinking.

"Only way to find out is to keep going," Ronald answered, and they continued.

Ronald was glad they had kept going that direction when what they heard turned out to be the most beautiful waterfall Ronald had ever seen.

"Beautiful!" George said as the three of them looked up at the waterfall in awe.

"Wait for us! That way led to a dead end!" They heard

Lucas yell as he and the other men came running up to where the rest of the group stood. They stopped dead in their tracks when they saw the waterfall.

Before Arthur and Lucas could elaborate, Ronald started feeling a tingling up his body. *What is going on?* He couldn't control the tingling and was alarmed when he felt like he was no longer in control of his own body.

"Gentlemen, I'm feeling strange. Are any of you experiencing anything out of the normal?" Ronald wanted to make sure he wasn't the only one experiencing the tingling.

"I feel strange as well, Ronald," Matt spoke up.

Before anyone else could say anything, they all saw a bright light that had a faint red glow coming out of an alcove off the central area of the cave.

"What in the world could that be?" Arthur's voice shook with excitement and uncertainty.

Ronald's voice felt like it belonged to someone else as he started speaking. "Whatever it is, we need to check it out." Ronald felt a strange connection with something in the alcove and was drawn to the light. The strange sensations kept happening as he ambled toward the opening.

George disagreed. "I vote we get out of here. This feeling is not normal."

Despite George's concerns, Ronald walked over to the alcove. On the wall outside the entrance, he saw some paintings of what he assumed were words in the Indian language: kdéde, ttą́nį sotté hi, hą́nąppáze, čʔa ttą́ka, and mą́t^{h}e.

Ronald felt fear trickling down his spine, and he wanted to turn around and run the other way, but his legs wouldn't obey him. Instead, he walked right in the alcove.

Once inside the alcove, he realized it was a large room and not an alcove after all. The walls had ancient-looking pots lined up all around the room. A couple of lanterns were hanging that Arthur and George lit.

Looking around the room, Ronald thought it looked like it had served as an Indian Chief's private quarters. He walked around the room, picking up various items he knew an Indian would use. It looked like someone had lived there and had one day up and abandoned everything.

That's when he saw the skeleton. It was arrayed in what had once been grand apparel, and there was a red velvet pouch with a red glow coming out of it clutched in the skeleton's hands. He realized he found the source of the light.

He couldn't stand it. He had to see what was inside the velvet pouch. Cautiously, he walked over to the skeleton and picked it up. He could feel power vibrating in his hands as he opened the cover.

From the moment he opened the pouch, everything happened in an instant. One second, he was looking in the pouch, and then the next, he was hit by a force so strong that it knocked him down.

As Ronald picked himself up off the ground, he understood two things. One, he no longer had full control of his own body, and two, the words he saw outside the entrance were a warning in the Quapaw Indian language meaning Run Fast and Escape, Dark, Evil Spirits Inside.

CHAPTER 1

Moon Lake, Arkansas
August 1995

Blood splattered on the floor and down the wall in James Edward Kensington's basement. He looked up at his assailant and smiled through bloody teeth. He felt a sense of relief with a touch of joy at finally finding out who had been behind the mystery that had consumed the last few weeks of his life.

Although James is unsure why he is so happy, he realized he would not make it out of the basement alive. He struggled against the leather straps that kept him bound to the chair.

"This is your last chance, Mr. Kensington." His assailant leered down at him, his ice-blue eyes seeming to shine in the dimly lit basement.

When James didn't flinch, his assailant leaned down even closer, his breath hitting James square in the face. "Tell me who else you have told of your little theories, and I may spare your life." James found it odd that his assailant's breath smelled like fresh strawberries mixed with smoke but knew it didn't matter at this point.

"Who else would I have told?" James cried. "There is no

one in my life anymore. You and your group of friends made sure of that!"

James jerked against the leather straps, but they didn't budge. He could feel the thin leather cutting into his wrists, but he didn't care. He jerked over and over until blood was dripping down his arms.

James felt that he was losing control as despair settled like a lead ball in the pit of his stomach. He prayed they never found out about Chrissy. Sweet Chrissy, who always had a ready smile and a kind word. She had been through so much and endured more loss in her short thirty years than anyone should ever have to. Even with that loss, she kept pushing forward and had made a good life for herself and her two girls. She hadn't been back home to Moon Lake in over fifteen years, but James made the trek to see them every few months.

The nightmare he had been living through all started when he stumbled upon a ten year old VHS tape wedged between his stove and cabinet. The kitchen faucet had a leak and caused James to have to tear some cabinets out due to the water. That is when he discovered the tape. It must have gotten knocked off the counter before he opened it.

After watching the tape, he started looking into his mother's death, and in doing that, he uncovered a string of disappearances that were somehow connected.

Then he started having nightmares about his mother being thrown down a hole while he watched, helpless to save her. In those dreams, he saw powerful magic being used and heard men talking about sacrificing people so they could stay powerful. He had not believed the dreams were memories until he walked into the Post Office one day and saw one of the men from his dream. Then he had thought the dreams could be memories that he had blocked out.

The nightmares/memories had made him more determined to find out what had happened to his mother and the rest of the people that had come up missing or murdered. His research intensified, and he even went to the Arkansas Times to see if they had any older articles about missing people from Moon Lake.

All his research had led him to believe that not only had this group of evil people killed his mother, but they had also killed his brother. Now he was next on their list.

His assailant slapped him across his face. "Snap out of it!" James could hear the impatience in his voice. He was getting more intense with the blows to James' head and upper body, and he knew the end was near.

"Would you at least tell me which one of you killed my mother and why? She never hurt anyone. How could her death have benefited your group?" James begged the man. "I know I won't be making it out of here alive, so it won't hurt your precious secret group to tell me."

His assailant leaned down and whispered, "She was scared during her last days on earth. She screamed and begged for mercy."

He got louder as he continued to speak, "Why do you think I came to your mother's funeral? Did you think I was kind, that I cared about your family's mourning? Not even a little! I had to make sure you and your brother didn't remember anything about the day your mother was sacrificed. Yes, James, you and your brother were both there and watched it all happen."

The assailant paused to grin down at James, gloating over what he was telling him. He enjoyed watching James suffer, and telling him what *really* happened was too much fun.

"I may as well let you in on a little secret about your father. He was a member of our "little group," as you like to call it. He was in on everything all along! He knew your mother had to die, and he did nothing to stop it! Your whole life has been a lie!" He laughed as if he had just heard the funniest joke in the world.

The shock was almost too much to bear as more memories

hit James, causing him to double over in pain. He leaned over against the chair and started dry heaving, begging for the pain of his memories to stop.

"This is not possible. You couldn't have killed my mother. You would be at least in your sixties now if you had killed her, and you clearly aren't. And why are you even talking about my father? I remember the day he left us after my mom died like it was yesterday. You are just trying to mess with my mind! None of this makes any sense."

Then James remembered those ice-blue eyes. He remembered the smell of strawberries mixed with smoke. It almost seemed like a dream.

Could this be real? Could this man have been there? Had he been the one to kill his mother? Could he be telling him the truth about his father? Regret filled James to the core as his assailant hit him across the face so hard the chair fell to the floor.

His last thought was of his niece, Chrissy. He had never gotten a chance to change his will. She and her children were the last living family he had, and years ago, he had made arrangements to leave everything he owned to Chrissy. But after his discovery of his mother's murder and the evil presence in Moon Lake, he had decided to exclude her from inheriting the Lodge and leave it to his best friend. He would leave Chrissy his monetary assets, but that had been all he planned on leaving her.

He had even scheduled an appointment with his attorney for that next week to make the changes official. He didn't want Chrissy and her daughters in Moon Lake and especially not living in the Lodge. Why had he waited? He had promised Allen he would take care of Chrissy.

His actions would bring Chrissy and her two sweet daughters here to this town. She had been safe living in Iowa for all these years. What had he done?

CHAPTER 2

C hrissy Bennett sighed as she clicked her blinker to turn left on Interstate 63, heading away from the town she had grown to love. She had moved to Burlington, Iowa, from a city outside Des Moines with her husband Dave right after graduating college. She and Dave had shared five wonderful years and had two beautiful daughters before a drunk driver had killed him in a horrific accident.

Sadness filled her with the thought of Dave. He had been her rock, her protector from all things, and the love of her life. He had been there to help her through the loss of her mother, and without him, she knew she would have ended up in a mental institute. Her despair had been so great after her mother vanished that she had almost shut down on life. Almost.

Dave had swooped in and given her life meaning. He helped her navigate her first week of college, and the rest was history.

She snuck a glance in her rear-view mirror and smiled at her eight-year-old, Lela, and her five-year-old, Jessica. Lela had taken after her daddy with her blonde curls and big blue eyes, while Jessica had inherited Chrissy's darker skin tone, brown eyes, and brown curls. Both girls were beautiful and had the attention of everyone no matter where they went.

Lela had been born Louise Helen Bennett but went by the nickname her dad had always called her. Her youngest was born

Jessica Rhnae Bennett, and she preferred to be called Jessica by everyone but Lela.

She was thankful she had opted to homeschool her girls. That sure made it easier to go back to Arkansas for a few weeks. She was an Interior Designer and was able to work mostly from home, so things worked out with the homeschooling.

Chrissy realized she was dealing with many issues and fears of losing her girls. She had lost so many people in her family, and she couldn't bear the thought of anything happening to her girls.

Jessica had something in her hand, and Chrissy couldn't quite make out what it was. "Mama," her oldest shrieked, "Jessi has a BUG!"

"Ha-ha! You're a scaredy-cat!" Jessica's giddy laughter was contagious, and they all laughed until Jessica decided she needed to go potty.

Chrissy was pumping gas after they finished using the bathroom and her mind wandered back to that phone call from the Friday before. She was still puzzled at what the attorney told her.

"Ms. Bennett, this is Roger Billings, your Uncle James Kensington's attorney. I am sorry to have to be the one to tell you, but your uncle James has passed away. You are his last known living relative, and some arrangements need to be finalized. Your Uncle James took care of his burial details a few years back, and he has requested a simple ceremony in the garden at The Lodge where he lived. It will be up to you as far as when you want to have the memorial service. When can you come to Moon Lake, Arkansas, to meet with me and finalize the details of your Uncle's last will and testament?"

Her mind snapped back to the present when Lela pecked on the window. Chrissy looked in at them, and her heart melted as both girls made heart shapes with their hands and blew her a kiss. She leaned over and kissed the glass, and both girls cackled when it fogged up.

The drive from Burlington to Moon Lake would take them around eight hours, so she planned on splitting it up over two days. About five hours was all the girls could do without having a throwdown in the back seat.

A few hours later, she was relieved to make it to the half-way point of Tea, Missouri. The welcome sign for the Holiday Inn beamed and blinked at her as she slowed down to turn in the drive.

She was thankful that she had already called and rented a room since she was mentally drained and knew her girls had to be beyond ready to get out of the car.

Chrissy pulled into the parking lot and unloaded their overnight bag before helping the girls out of the Tahoe. It was then that she got an eerie feeling of being watched. Chrissy scanned the parking lot, and nothing seemed to be out of place. She decided it was the fatigue of the long drive and stress of the past week making her paranoid, so they made their way to the Hotel Lobby to get checked in.

Henry Kesselburg opened his trunk and got out his leather bag, doing his best to act normal and keep his head down. Chrissy Bennett had almost caught him watching her as she got her girls out of the back seat. He wondered how he could have let that happen.

If he was honest with himself, he knew how he let it happen. He had gotten caught off guard by how beautiful he found Chrissy Bennett. He had known her when she was a child, and he had even seen pictures of her as an adult hanging on James's wall, but nothing had prepared him for the instant attraction he felt.

That was an amateur mistake! He mentally kicked himself again. Was there something else that had caused him to let his guard down? He reminded himself that he was no amateur when it came to hiding in plain sight. Indeed, he had plenty of practice remaining unseen as he tracked and followed people. One hundred eight years, to be exact.

He had watched many people over the years and had never been noticed. Did he mention the people he usually watched were vampires, and most had super keen senses? So how could he let a human almost catch him watching her?

The bulk of his time was spent saving humans from rogue vampires. Rogue vampires fed on humans with no care for human life, and that sickened Henry. He despised all they stood for. How could they not care for human life? How could they forget they were once humans themselves?

Henry had set up Vampire Covens in every major city across the United States and had plans to eventually set up at least one Vampire Coven in every country outside the United States. The Vampires Coven were managed and led by an Elder. They met with Henry once a quarter to discuss the state of Vampirism in their area and their plans to keep human casualties at a minimum.

Henry felt very strongly about keeping humans as safe as possible, which gave him a purpose to keep going. He had found one woman he thought he could eventually grow to love, but it turned out to be a scam.

Johanna had lied to Henry from the start, and he didn't see it. She claimed to be sympathetic to humans for the sole purpose of getting inside the Coven Henry had been staying with in Atlanta, Georgia. But, turned out, Johanna was a Rogue Vampire who had a vendetta against the man Henry had in charge of The Agency, Miguel Sanchez. Johanna blamed Miguel for the death of her brother.

Henry had confronted Johanna after she attacked Miguel one night when she caught him alone. Luckily, Miguel had been able to subdue her without causing her too much injury until help arrived.

She had snuck off that night, and Henry had not seen her since. He couldn't believe that it had been over fifty years since he had seen her face. He was now just thankful she hadn't caused any more problems.

After Johanna used him, he closed his heart off and focused solely on helping people. That was all he needed out of life. At least, that is what he made himself believe.

He let out a breath when he saw the trio disappear into the lobby. He didn't realize he had been holding his breath until he was positive Chrissy Bennett didn't see his face. He had been an immortal for over a century and never gotten out of the habit of breathing like a human. Not that he had tried.

After giving Chrissy Bennett plenty of time to get checked in, Henry went in and paid for a room. He had no intention of staying in the room overnight but would use it to freshen up after his overnight shift of guard duty. He wasn't even sure who would be following her, but he knew that her Uncle James wanted him to protect Chrissy and her daughters so he would not allow anything to happen to that family. Not on his watch.

CHAPTER 3

Henry eased out of the hotel parking lot, allowing a few cars to get between him and the SUV. He figured they would arrive in Moon Lake around noon if they kept the same pace as the day before.

He got lost in thought, thinking about a conversation from a few short days earlier as he cruised along.

The person he trusted most with his life had warned him of evil in the town he lived. *"Henry, I have come to believe there is a presence at Moon Lake that does not belong. I have dreams of my mother's death and can't put them out of my mind. I keep dreaming that a cult sacrificed my mother. The men in this cult have strange powers, and somehow, they must sacrifice people to keep those powers. I have come to believe these dreams are memories. Memories I have suppressed for years. Henry, my mother, was murdered by these people and sacrificed so they can stay powerful. Nothing will ever convince me that she wasn't. I just need to figure out why. Why her."*

Henry interrupted James to ask a couple of questions, "James, I thought your mother died in a freak accident. Is it only your dreams that make you think she was murdered? How long have you been going through this, and why are you only calling me now?"

"I haven't called you because I wanted to make sure that I wasn't losing my mind first. Initially, I believed the dreams were simply dreams. I blamed the dreams on my finding a VHS tape that I had

misplaced without watching years earlier. But after spending time researching, I discovered that there is a pattern of people either dying or disappearing right here in Moon Lake, and no one can explain it. My mother was somehow connected to the cult that I keep dreaming about, but I can't remember how. Her death has always been a mystery that I couldn't solve, and I am getting closer to solving the mystery surrounding not only her death but also my brother's death and my father's disappearance." Henry could hear James's voice shaking over the phone.

"Please tell me how I can help with this, James."

"After watching the video, I started searching the woods on my property and came across an old cabin where I found something I don't understand. The cabin is very well hidden, and I had forgotten it was even there. I have not taken the time to hike that far into the woods since I was a kid. Maybe I should have. Maybe I could have put a stop to this evil sooner if I had. I don't want to go into the details over the phone, but please believe me when I tell you that whatever is going on here is not normal. There is something evil here. An evil that I can't take care of alone. I need help from someone who is strong and who can't be easily killed. Henry, I need your help here."

Henry could feel the urgency coming through the phone, "I will pack my bags and leave Los Angeles first thing in the morning. I can be there tomorrow afternoon, James." Henry answered.

"Thank you. And Henry, if anything ever happens to me, please watch over my niece and her two girls."

"I give you my word that I will watch over them. But I don't plan on anything happening to you, buddy." Henry had promised he would watch over them. And he would.

"Thank you. You can't know how much this means to me." James sounded so thankful.

"See you in a couple of days."

"Until then."

That was the last time he had spoken to James Edward Kensington. His friend had been found dead the very next morning by the man who worked for him as Property Manager. The paramedics said he was unresponsive when they arrived, and he was pronounced dead then and there. The Medical Examiner cited "natural causes" on his death certificate. Henry didn't believe for a moment that he had died of natural causes.

He had searched the lodge that James owned and could feel the fear James had felt during his last moments. Henry knew he had been tortured and killed right there in his basement. *What is going on here? People don't get tortured and killed for nothing. Could there be a cult right here in Moon Lake like James suspected?* Henry had thought to himself. He had to have been right when he said he was close to solving the mystery around his mother's death. Someone had to have found out James had been about to figure things out and had him killed. But who? And why? The cult?

James's mother had been a stay-at-home mom when she was killed. What possible reason could the person who killed her have for also killing her son years later? Unless James was right. Unless there truly is a cult in Moon Lake.

Henry had known James's niece would come to Moon Lake when she found out about her Uncle's death, so he left The Lodge and drove straight through to Iowa. He wasn't sure what was happening, but he knew there was a chance she and her family would be in danger. She would certainly be in trouble if the cult leaders saw her as a threat. He would have to stick close to Chrissy Bennett and her girls. He had made a promise to keep them safe, and he would live up to that promise. For James.

The quarter he had in his pocket bent as Henry clutched it between his fingers. He kept a fresh quarter there in case he felt the need to break something. After replacing his windshield a few times, he had learned his lesson. Not that he had anger issues, he just grew angry when people were killed unjustly. And he knew for a fact that James had been killed unjustly.

He never had killed anyone without reason and never would. He appreciated life and felt that others should as well.

Henry had been turned into a Vampire when he was thirty-eight years old. By his own mother. She felt she didn't have a choice as he had been shot then trampled by a horse when he was out for a ride one day. The man who had shot him thought he was an escaped convict and didn't realize his mistake until after he fell off his horse. The man had carried him straight to his mother when he realized who he was.

Henry remembered that day like it was yesterday. *"I am so sorry; I was hunting the wretched man who escaped and mistook Henry for him. Please save him!"* Their neighbor, Adolphus Baumgart, had begged for Katarina to save Henry.

Henry knew he was fortunate that his neighbor was a sympathizer to Vampires. He had helped them farm their land and was fond of both Katarina and Henry.

She had saved his life, and he was grateful to her for it. Even though the pain was almost unbearable. Henry had felt her strong venom travel down his throat and hit his heart like a grenade. After he had transformed, they had to flee from Germany to America.

He was so incredibly grateful to have the life he did. He knew that decision was not an easy one for his mother to make. She had known the agony he would go through, but she couldn't bear losing her only son.

Henry grew up hearing stories about the Grand Vampire Elder, who lived amongst the humans but never believed them. Not until it had killed his father and left his mother alive but wounded in the woods a few miles from their home. Henry had only just turned twenty-one and had been on holiday celebrating with his friends when his parents had been attacked. He had lived with the guilt of not being there for them ever since.

After she turned, his mother had moved them to another part of Germany and had tried her best to continue being the loving mother and person she always had been. He knew it hadn't been the easiest time for her, but she had been determined not to let the evil that someone had done to her ruin their lives.

After Henry became an Immortal, they had moved to America and started The Agency, spending their days helping keep humans safe from Rogue Vampires.

That is until his mother traveled back to Germany the previous year. She had a score to settle with the vampire who had killed her husband. She wanted answers, and she wanted revenge in the form of his head.

Henry wanted to join her on her hunt, but she had forbidden him from going. Even though he didn't want her hunting the Grand Vampire Elder alone, he would respect her wishes. And she had promised not to engage him without backup from their Vampire coven in Germany, so he felt better about the situation. His mother had never lied to him or broken a promise, and he didn't expect her to start now.

Jerking his mind back to the present, he wondered about what could be happening in Moon Lake. *Who could be behind his friend's death? The cult leader? What did James mean by evil powers?*

Henry had found a piece of paper with a partial list that James had marked with years and names. The years started as early as 1939 and ended in 1976, and some of the years had question marks by them, while others had names. What did this mean? He knew he would have to do more research when he arrived at the Lodge.

He looked up in time to see Chrissy Bennett pull into a Bonanza a few miles outside of Moon Lake. It was a little after eleven, so he figured they were ready for lunch. Not willing to be seen in the same restaurant, he decided to pull one of his meals out of his ice chest. Henry preferred rare steak above anything else and was looking forward to his meal.

Almost an hour later, they were back on the road heading right into Moon Lake, Arkansas. If only they knew what awaited them there, they might have turned around and never looked back.

CHAPTER 4

"I'm thirsty!" Jessica announced as they passed the sign that proclaimed a population of 27,800 for Moon Lake. Chrissy hoped the Lodge Restaurant was open or at least had makings for sandwiches for dinner so she wouldn't have to go to the grocery store before morning. Her bones ached, and she knew her girls were worn out, so a trip to the store would have to wait until the next day unless the restaurant was closed.

The town looked the same. Chrissy was blown away by how nothing had changed. Although she had to admit it was a welcoming sight.

Historic buildings lined Main Street, and the shops were decorated so that it almost transported locals and visitors alike back in time. The roads were all light red brick and reminded Chrissy of the town in Italy she and Dave had gone to on their honeymoon. The main attraction, though, was the park that was situated right in the middle of town. Everyone loved how it led to the lake that was on the outskirts of the town.

She wondered if Mr. Gus was still alive. He rented boats so people could paddle around in the narrow part of the lake. She used to beg her daddy to take her to visit Mr. Gus, and he always ended up renting a boat so they could paddle around. What good memories those were. Some of the best with just her and her daddy.

Chrissy glanced over at the fog sitting on top of the lake like a second skin and thought it was beautiful in an eerie way. She couldn't help but think of her parents, and the few short years they spent together on that very lake.

They had been such a happy family until her daddy left to go hunting one Saturday morning when she was twelve and never returned. She had been fourteen years old when a hunter had uncovered his body two years later in a remote wooded area. That had been the beginning of the end with her mother's mental health.

Her mother moved them to a suburb outside of Des Moines, Iowa, and had never looked back. At least Chrissy thought she hadn't. Chrissy had just graduated high school when her mother disappeared. It's like she had never existed. One day her mom was there smiling as Chrissy was graduating high school, then within a month, she was gone. Along with all her things – like she never even existed.

Chrissy had gotten a job at Burger King before starting college to help keep her mind busy and give her some spending money. Luckily, her mom had bought their house with cash from her dad's life insurance policy, so she didn't have to worry about a place to live. The little money left over and her scholarship had gotten her by until she graduated college.

The police had come up empty-handed in their search. After a year, the case was considered cold. Everyone assumed her mother had run off with a man or was dead. But Chrissy knew better.

Chrissy had hired a private investigator after graduating from college and was making money, but he had not found her trail either.

Regret and sadness filled Chrissy's heart, and she quickly blinked away the tear that silently fell down her cheek. She missed her parents. She missed her uncle. She longed for Dave to hold her and give her that comfort he always had before that drunk driver took him away from them. She wanted to curl up in a ball and cry for all that she had lost. *Snap out of it, Chrissy. You are blessed to have two healthy, beautiful children. There are a lot of people who are not so fortunate.* She mentally chastised herself.

She decided to think about happy things until they reached the drive for The Lodge. When she saw the turnoff, she smiled as the memories of her childhood started flowing. Thankfully, her childhood memories were mostly good ones before her dad had been killed.

As she pulled in, she tried to take it all in at once. Especially the flowers. They were so beautiful. Purple Echinacea lined the front of the lodge along with other vibrant plants, flowers, and bushes. The Lodge was primarily made of logs but had rock and stone incorporated in the building material. Large glass windows lined the front of the lodge that made it seem even more extensive than it was. If you pulled in at the right spot, you could see the lake out of the windows in the back of the lodge by looking in the front windows. It was a straight shot.

"Girls look through the front windows," she wanted them to see how beautiful it was. She looked up at the roof and remembered playing for hours in the attic. She would always pretend to be a beautiful princess in her castle. The attic had the perfect setup for little girls with active imaginations.

She glanced at the Tool Shed as she pulled through the driveway and felt a tinge of another memory. A memory that she quickly pushed to the back of her mind. For some reason, that was a memory she didn't want to deal with or even remember. *Maybe she could deal with it later, she thought. Maybe.*

There was always something to get into at The Lodge. She hoped her girls had as much fun here as she had when she was a little girl.

Chrissy was determined to focus on the good memories and give her girls a good time while they were visiting. She knew that wouldn't be easy, especially under the circumstances, but she would sure try.

She noticed an older couple walking towards her as she started unloading her Tahoe and smiled at them. The man looked to be in his early sixties; he was of medium height, well-built, and silver hair cut close to his scalp. The woman looked to be a few years younger. She had black hair that was cut in a bob and suited her rounded face.

"Welcome to The Lodge," the gentleman said as he stuck his hand out. "You must be Christina Bennett. You were just a young girl the last time we saw you. I'm Geoffrey Hamilton, and this is my wife, Rose. I manage the property, and Rose runs the restaurant here at The Lodge. We've been expecting you."

"Please, you can call me Chrissy." She was not a fan of people calling her Christina. Her full name was Christina Elizabeth Kensington Bennett, and it just sounded too formal. And since she was not a particularly formal person, she liked the more mellow sound of Chrissy. Plus, that is what her daddy called her, and it made her feel closer to him keeping that name.

They discussed James and how they all were so sorry when he passed away before spending a few minutes exchanging pleasantries. Rose even insisted on a hug from her and the girls. They made her feel welcomed and like she had come home from a long vacation. She found out that The Lodge was temporarily closed due to the circumstances with James passing, but Miss Rose still had the kitchen open and a roast in the oven for supper.

They dropped their bags in a large suite that overlooked the lake. Chrissy stood still for a moment, looking at the beautiful fall colors in the trees and watching the water flow. The water brought back memories of jumping off the dock and swimming like a fish, of barbecues with her family, and happy childhood moments.

"Girls, this is the lake I swam in as a girl. What do y'all think about swimming while we are here while it's still warm enough?"

The girls jumped up and down to show their excitement, and both said, "Yeah!"

Chrissy stopped to enjoy another beautiful view of the lake and outdoor garden in the vast Great Room. It was apparent the garden had been a labor of love by many others who had come before her. It had a walkway filled with arches and beautiful blooms of different flowers and plants that bloomed at different times based on the seasons. There were several benches strategically placed that allowed guests to have the best views possible.

She looked around the Great Room and decided it was perfect. The earth-toned furniture was a little worn but looked highly comfortable as it was extensive with a lot of cushions. She did love how a large table sat in the corner of the room for guests to eat or play games on. It was a table with a view! That was a smart move. Her Uncle James must have added that piece after she and her mom had moved.

Her favorite part of the room had to be the area around the fireplace. The fireplace of large stones matched the stones on the outside of the lodge. The fireplace went from the floor to the ceiling, and there was a beautifully handmade box that stored wood at the bottom of the fireplace.

Directly next to the fireplace were glass windows that went all the way to the ceiling. There were built-in benches with green cushions and several colorful throw pillows that allowed guests to sit and enjoy the view while reading or simply relaxing. Dividing the benches was a beautiful wood beam that also stretched to the ceiling. The beam was stained brown and tied in perfectly with the wood box.

Chrissy was amazed by the view and laughed when Lela and Jessica settled in on one of the benches. "Come on to the kitchen, girls, let's get a glass of tea."

A few hours later, Chrissy and her girls were settled in

their room, bellies full and partially unpacked. She stood in front of the mirror, looking at her reflection and trying to figure out what felt off about the situation with her Uncle's death.

Other than sounding stressed, her Uncle James sounded perfectly healthy the last time they spoke, which had only been a month or so earlier. He promised Chrissy he was fine and had blamed a water leak and having to replace cabinets as his source of stress, so Chrissy hadn't thought much more about it.

Then there was Moon Lake. She had an eerie feeling about the town. She couldn't put her finger on it but knew she wouldn't be able to rest until she figured it out.

◆ ◆ ◆

Henry drove past The Lodge and pulled into the driveway to his cabin. He had bought the place from James in 1970 and used it as his home away from home. He and James had met in the summer of '63 in Destin, Florida. They had both booked a day of deep-sea fishing and had hit it off rather quickly. Henry had sensed deep despair coming from James and had felt a quick connection to him. They ended up going deep-sea fishing together three times that week and committed to meet up in Destin for an annual fishing trip.

James was the best friend he had been looking for and needing in his life. Not that he even realized he was looking. He and James had several things in common and had bonded over those things. They had both suffered loss, yet they were both easy-going; both had never married, but the thing that brought them the closest was their love of catching fish on the open water.

Henry thought back to the day he confided in James. It was ten years after they met when he had decided to trust James fully. He told him the whole story of his immortality one evening after an enjoyable day of catching fish in the middle of the ocean. James has bagged two Mahi-mahi, four redfish, and a few Grouper while Henry had landed a shark. Not that he kept it. He sure wanted to, though. That day went down as one of his favorite days.

James wasn't surprised or shocked by the news that his friend was an immortal. What made Henry know he made the right decision was that nothing changed between them. James hadn't treated him any differently. The first time he asked anything extra from Henry was when he suspected an evil in Moon Lake and asked for his help, which had only been recent.

Henry was aware that James had lost his mother at a young age and that his father had run off shortly after she died, but they had never discussed it in detail. James had said that his mother had been killed in a freak accident, and his father left James and his brother, Allen. Henry had not ever pushed for more information and figured James would bring it up if he wanted to talk.

Henry was determined to finish what James started. He would figure out what was happening in Moon Lake, and he would make sure James's niece and her children stayed safe.

CHAPTER 5

C hrissy and her girls made it down to breakfast a little before eight o'clock, and Ms. Rose was there, ready to greet them with a smile and hug. The Dining Room was large yet cozy. It was filled with homemade tables and chairs made using local logs, and the walls were decorated with mounted fish, old boats, oars, and nets. That wouldn't have been Chrissy's first choice for decoration, but it worked. It more than worked. It looked inviting and somehow calmed Chrissy's nerves.

As expected, the restaurant was empty other than one table. A man was sitting at it, but he had his back to her, so she wasn't sure if she knew him or not. All she could see was dark brown hair and what looked to be a muscular build.

The girls settled on pancakes and milk while Chrissy was in the mood for coffee only. She couldn't let her nerves get her too worked up. She had a meeting scheduled with the attorney at eleven o'clock and wanted to put her best foot forward. She knew it wouldn't do her any good to arrive frazzled.

After getting her coffee all doctored up, Chrissy saw that Ms. Rose was visiting with the man at the other table. They seemed to be deep in conversation, and they were speaking so low that Chrissy couldn't hear what they were talking about.

Jessica chose that moment to loudly ask, "Ms. Rose! Can I please have some chocolate chips to go with my pancakes?"

Both Ms. Rose and the gentleman turned in their direction, and Chrissy felt herself blush at being caught staring. Strangely, she felt her blush deepen when the man smiled at Jessica. Could men be called beautiful? If so, he would fit the bill.

He had dark brown hair, and his blue eyes danced with what Chrissy would call light mischievousness. His nose and eyebrows were placed in the most perfect places on his face. *Stop it!* She told herself. *Stop staring. Just stop.*

When he met her gaze, he lifted one eyebrow and grinned like he could hear her heart beating out of her chest.

Oh no. Chrissy thought to herself. This couldn't be happening. She didn't find men attractive anymore. Not that she couldn't. She just wouldn't by choice. It had only been three years since they had lost Dave, and she had no intention of putting her girls through that again.

Henry couldn't help but smile when he felt all the different emotions running through Chrissy. She found him attractive! But she was not happy about it.

He took a minute to study her face after she moved her attention to Ms. Rose. She was a beautiful woman. That was a given. Her jet-black hair hung in loose curls down her back, her skin was a medium tone, she had big brown eyes and a genuine and honest smile. She had a friendly face like her uncle, which made him like her right from the start. Her Uncle was blonde and fair-skinned, so Henry figured she must take after her mother with her exotic darker complexion.

Deciding to get the inevitable over, he walked up to her table and introduced himself. He turned to the girls first, "Hi there, young ladies, I'm Heinrich, but you can call me Henry. You must be Lela and Jessica."

"How do you know our names?" Lela asked as she accepted the bag of chocolate chips from Ms. Rose.

"I thought all the pretty young ladies were named Lela and Jessica!" Henry replied. He wasn't sure what all he should say about his relationship with James. Better to avoid the question altogether.

Chrissy found her voice and joined the conversation, "Are you any relation to the Henry my uncle was so close to?"

When he got up close, she thought he looked a lot like her Uncle James's best friend that she had met when she was a kid.

Maybe he was a relative of Henry's. He must be. He even had the same name, so he was more than likely his son. She didn't remember ever meeting a son, but that didn't mean anything.

"You could say that." Henry's voice snapped her back to the conversation. "I own a cabin on the far corner of the property. We have grown close over the years, and I was so sorry to hear of his passing. Please don't hesitate to let me know if I can do anything to help you while you're here." Henry thought he had never been able to say the right thing during times of loss.

Chrissy felt he was evasive but chose to keep her thoughts to herself. "Thank you. I'm Chrissy, by the way. It's nice to meet you, Henry." He was even better looking up close and personal. *Stop that*, she said to herself.

"Have you made the arrangements yet?" Henry asked Chrissy. "I want to make sure I don't miss the memorial service."

Before Chrissy could answer Henry, Jessica piped in.

"Mommy! Are you hot? Your face is redddd!" Jessica seemed to think she needed to talk loud enough for the neighbors down the road to hear.

"Honey, you need to finish your pancakes, so we're not late for our appointment." Chrissy decided she would ignore the uncomfortable line of questioning from her daughter.

"But Mommy, you didn't ans..." Jessica started to protest when Chrissy ignored her questions, but Lela cut her off. "She's ignoring you, silly!"

Chrissy took the opportunity to stand up and start cleaning the table off, hoping that Jessica would let it go. Henry began to help, and thankfully the moment passed. "I plan on having Uncle James's funeral Tuesday morning at ten o'clock in the garden here."

"I will be there," Henry replied, "Please let me know if you need my help with anything. I am in the last cabin down the gravel road on the left."

"Henry, it was nice meeting you." Chrissy smiled up at him in thanks for letting the subject drop and for offering to help her.

"It was nice meeting you, three lovely ladies. I'm sure we will see each other again soon." Henry smiled back at Chrissy and left the restaurant.

He knew he would have to be extremely careful, or Chrissy Bennett would steal his heart.

CHAPTER 6

T he ride home from the lawyer's office was almost a blur. She still was in shock that her Uncle James left her The Lodge and all his other assets. She should have expected it with her being his only living family, but for some reason, she hadn't. Her mind whirled at the thought of leaving her home in Iowa. But could she turn her back on The Lodge?

After she graduated college, she had gone to work for a minor design firm in Burlington and had worked there until she got pregnant with Lela. After taking some time off from work, she and Dave had decided to include an office for her at his Landscaping business to conduct business around home design. It had been successful as Dave already had a large existing customer base. Once Chrissy had come on board using the same office building, several had used her for different design opportunities.

It would be a hard decision for Chrissy to make. Moon Lake was the home she had with her parents. This place held so many memories for her of her youth. But on the other hand, Iowa held memories of her time with Dave and her mother after her father died.

She knew she would have to make a list of her pros and cons before deciding. It wasn't about the money, but she also needed to go through the books for The Lodge. She needed to make sure she could support her family and have enough to pay for her girls to go to college. Her Uncle James had over a hundred thousand in the bank, which was huge, and the attorney sent a list of the assets to go through. She decided to worry about finances after the funeral and not rush into a decision. Better to take her time and make sure she was doing the right thing.

Chrissy and her girls had spent time getting to know the Property Manager and his wife after breakfast, and her girls had quickly taken to them both. Dave's parents lived in Florida, and the girls only got to see them a few times a year, but she knew they missed having them around more often. Geoffrey and Rose reminded her of Dave's parents. They were both very loving couples who seemed to have a lot of patience with kids.

Chrissy was looking forward to getting to know them better. She remembered their kindness when she was a little girl and was happy they were still working at The Lodge.

Chrissy, Lela, and Jessica spent the next few days getting to know Geoffrey and Rose and spending quality time together. Henry had come around at least once every day, but he seemed like he wanted to keep more to himself. Chrissy told herself it didn't matter to her whether he came around more. It's not like she wanted to get to know him better.

On the day of the funeral, Chrissy and the girls got ready and went to breakfast a little before 9 o'clock. She had allowed them to sleep in since she knew it would be a very long, hard day for them all.

Henry was already there with his cup of coffee, reading the paper. "Good morning, ladies."

"Morning, Mr. Henry!" The girls danced in, singing a greeting.

"Good morning," Chrissy responded as she noticed that Henry was not eating again. "Not hungry again, Henry?"

"Something like that. I am more of a coffee drinker in

the morning," he answered vaguely and continued sipping his coffee. He had never been able to stop drinking coffee. Not that he had tried. He loved it, and human food didn't hurt him. It just wouldn't sustain him. "Were you able to get any rest?"

"A little. I kept rehearsing what I will be saying at the service today. Uncle James was such a good man, and I want to make sure I get that across to everyone in attendance."

"I have faith in you." Henry grabbed her hand and briefly squeezed it.

Chrissy was thankful for his support. Even though she had only known him for a few days, it felt like a lot longer. Deep down, she knew it had been a lot longer. "I appreciate your kind words."

"I'm not saying them to be kind." Henry looked at Chrissy, almost imploring her to believe in herself. "I meant every word."

Chrissy felt her heartbeat start to race. *I am not interested in a relationship with anyone right now. Especially with someone, she was suspicious of hiding something. Even someone as kind and wonderful as Henry. Stop it.*

"Morning Henry. Morning Chrissy." Geoffrey greeted them both as he came out of the kitchen with a pan of Cinnamon Rolls.

"That smells gooooood!" Lela exclaimed, and Jessica readily agreed, "Mmmm-hmmm."

"Help yourselves." Geoffrey offered as he put the platter on the table. "Save some room, though. I will be right back with some bacon and eggs!"

Chrissy followed him to the kitchen, "Let me help you, Geoffrey."

They both returned with platters of eggs, bacon, biscuits while Rose carried a bowl of gravy and a jar of Strawberry Jam.

"Whoa!" Jessica beamed. "This is a lot of food!"

"Rose doesn't know how to cook a small meal. Not that I'm complaining." Geoffrey said as he patted his belly,

"Well, let's eat," Rose added, "we don't want the food to get cold."

Chrissy noticed Henry with a cinnamon roll and felt guilty for pushing him about not eating. *Quit looking for something to be wrong with him, Chrissy. You are only doing that because you find him attractive. No, I don't. Yes, you do. Quit lying to yourself.* She sometimes had arguments in her head. At least she had started since meeting Henry.

After breakfast, everyone got cleaned up before heading down to the garden for James's memorial service.

◆ ◆ ◆

"Chrissy, you have sure done your Uncle James proud today." Rose praised Chrissy as they made their way up the pathway from the garden back to The Lodge.

"I agree," Geoffrey added.

"He would have appreciated your words so much. You let everyone in attendance know how much he meant to you. Not only to you but to others. He was a very giving man." Henry agreed with Rose and Geoffrey.

"Thank you. I can't tell you three how much I appreciate you three. The support you have all shown me has helped get me through this."

"Mommy, I need to use the bathroom," Jessica informed everyone.

"Ok, honey. Remember, we are going swimming before lunch." Chrissy said to both girls. Then looked at Geoffrey, Rose, and Henry. "You are all more than welcome to join us."

Henry and Geoffrey both declined, saying they had work to do.

"I would love to join you!" Rose smiled, happy to spend time with Chrissy and the girls. "I made some Chicken Salad sandwiches this morning for our lunch, so I have plenty of time to enjoy this beautiful day."

"Sounds good. Give us ten minutes, and we will meet you at the dock." Chrissy said as Jessica grabbed her hand to run the rest of the distance to The Lodge with Henry and Lela close behind them.

CHAPTER 7

R onald Burgess cracked his knuckles before getting into his black Mercedes. He had taken no pleasure in what he had done that night but felt he had no choice. Someone was trying to take over as head of The Council, and he would not allow that to happen.

He *could not* allow that to happen. No one else would have the same goals as Ronald. He wanted what was best for all the people in their Community. He would do everything he could to be the leader he was supposed to be. No one else would. He was convinced.

He looked at his reflection in the rear-view mirror, liking what he saw. He knew he was a good-looking man with his blond hair, blue eyes, and muscular build – the women, had made that clear over the years. He never had trouble getting anyone he set his sights on.

Except for one woman. The one woman he wanted more than anything. She didn't give him a second glance for years until he removed all obstacles. No matter that one of those obstacles happened to be his grandson. *Enough of that line of thought.*

Ronald suspected that Bradley was trying to take his place as head of the Council – he must be, or he would not have made such a decision without coming to Ronald first. How Bradley could have forgotten that Ronald was in charge was beyond him.

Killing Bradley Whitmore had simply been unavoidable due to Bradley's own stupidity. He had forced Ronald's hand when he killed the only grandson he had left without permission. Did he expect that there wouldn't be consequences? Ronald understood James had been researching the Council, and he was glad of it. After much thought, Ronald had decided that James would be honored with a spirit of his own. Ronald liked the idea of having his grandson living with him as an Immortal. But that would never happen now.

The Council Members had a responsibility to keep the Community safe and keep The Ancient One in sacrifices. If not, the world would end as everyone knew it. He had to admit that he had done a great job so far, and now that there were only a couple of months left, so he had to stay focused on the task at hand now more than ever.

Even though it had been almost two hundred years, he remembered the night the Ancient One honored him with communication like it was yesterday. He couldn't believe it when the spirit entered his body and revealed its plans to him. Not to the others. To him! Plans on returning to the Earth and spreading joy to those who are worthy. Plans it asked Ronald to oversee. The Ancient One had agreed that no one was better suited for the job than Ronald.

The Ancient One had been busy using the sacrifices to create more spirits to be released on the Earth. After the Ultimate Sacrifice, they would be released to meld with only those deemed worthy. Worthy of immortality. Worthy of a servant leadership role under Ronald and The Ancient One.

Ronald didn't even mind sharing his body with the spirit. As long as it kept him immortal, it didn't matter a lot to him. He wouldn't be greedy. He had long hoped The Ancient One would choose him to meld with, and he was confident that would happen in the end. Especially after seeing all Ronald was willing to do for the cause. The Ancient One would need a body when it returned to Earth, and who better to meld with than Ronald? *No one.*

Just thinking about The Ancient One being released from its prison made him smile. Within a couple of months, there would be peace on Earth. The Ancient One would move the unworthy and the ones who didn't belong far away from the blessed and worthy. They would stay there until it was time to use their life force for sacrifice to The Ancient One. Most of them wouldn't even realize they lived for feeding The Ancient One. That was a more humane way to handle things.

Ronald knew that would allow those who did belong to live happier, more peaceful lives. Lives that didn't end for the ones lucky enough to be melded with a spirit. He couldn't wait!

It was his job to stop anyone threatening their future by any means necessary.

He felt a burst of anger hit him and had to calm himself down before pulling out of the drive. He sensed there was something else causing his emotional state to be almost uncontrollable, but he could not put his finger on it, so he pushed the feeling aside.

He reminded himself again that everything he had done and would do was for a reason. For the greater good. For his Community. For the believers and for those who would come to believe.

Ronald knew he could not allow his emotions to get in the way. He needed to be entirely in control of his feelings so he could take care of his enemies. To ensure his enemies would not hurt his future wife and the plans he had made. He planned on living with her forever, and no one would ever get in his way.

He would have to find out if anyone else on The Council was plotting against him. Robert Vines was the newest Member and hadn't even completed a cycle yet. Ronald didn't think he had the guts to try to take over, so he moved on to the next newest member, Anthony Hightower.

Anthony had taken Geoffrey's place after he died. Ronald

didn't think Anthony would plot against him, but he wasn't entirely sure.

George Watkins and Lucas Rollings had been members of The Council since day one. Those were men he would need to keep close so he could keep an eye on them. They could be working together to take over. Ronald hated the thought but knew he would take steps to remove them as well if necessary.

He also needed six more people to add to those for the final sacrifice. Everything was coming together, and he could not allow his anger to get the best of him. Not when he was so close.

So close to melding with the Spirit living inside him. Knowing that once they truly become one, he would be a full-fledged Immortal. No more constantly worrying about dying.

October 31st would make two hundred years since his life changed for the better. He was a good man and was even better after being given a purpose. He knew he was a good man because he always ensured The Council chose worthless people. People who were a blight to society. Vagrants, liars, runaways, evil people. They needed to be taken out anyway, right?

The other sacrifices were necessary. Ronald didn't like to think about those that were required to continue the cycle. These were the hard sacrifices. The people he loved. His family. It had never gotten easier over the years.

Enough! He thought to himself. *Thinking about those sacrifices can do no good. It was better to block them out.*

It was time to set up a meeting to figure out who he and The Council would be picking for the six needed sacrifices. He planned on taking three per month so people would not be as suspicious. Those from town and a few more people already living in The Community, and they would be set.

In the end, he knew the police department would blame their disappearances on wild animal attacks or falling off the dam.

As mayor, he had set up a committee dedicated to keeping

wild animals safe and out of populated areas in Moon Lake. That was why he spent so much time searching the woods, because of his dedication to keeping the wild animals safe. Or so the people thought.

They had over one hundred people disappear over the past fifty years, even more before then. People had been quick to believe that the disappearances were due to their negligence. They agreed that people needed to be more careful in the woods and needed to stay away from the dam.

If only the citizens of Moon Lake knew the truth. They would never see those missing people again. Or at least they had better hope they never saw them again. For their own sakes.

CHAPTER 8

hey had been there almost two months, and Chrissy had felt a peace within like she hadn't felt since Dave was alive. One Saturday morning, she woke up in the mood to go exploring The Lodge. She already knew the first place she wanted to go was the attic. She wondered if her secret spots were still secret and couldn't wait to find out! She knew the girls would be excited to be in on the "secret."

As they climbed the stairs, she noticed how clean everything was, and once they made it to the top, she saw the attic itself was a lot more organized than she remembered it ever being. She was surprised but happy it wasn't full of spiders and such!

Chrissy went straight to the windows and started knocking on the wooden floor directly under the window. She looked for a loose board and giggled when she was rewarded with the one-second closest to the wall popping up. She felt like a little kid again as she pulled out the tin container.

Hmmm, odd. There were two containers in her hiding spot. Her tin box was still there, and then there was another blue box that looked old and worn and was faded. She set it aside and grabbed the tin box. She heard both girls jumping up and down, unable to contain their excitement. She didn't blame them!

She carefully opened the lid, expecting to find a Barbie, a couple of pencils, some notes her friends had written, and some drawings. All things from her childhood.

41

Much to her surprise, the contents of that tin box had nothing to do with her childhood. Or at least she thought. She would find out later that the contents absolutely had everything to do with her childhood.

There was a stack of papers with dates and names. *That's odd,* she thought. Date of disappearance was also at the top under the name. What in the world?

She kept digging and found a gun, bullets, a VHS tape, another folder with some papers, and an envelope with her name on it.

The girls had lost interest when they saw her tin box contained what they thought was just a bunch of papers. She noticed they had their heads in the other box and they were for sure enthralled with whatever was inside.

She first examined a note taped on the outside and saw her uncle had noted that he found this box a few days prior in an old fallout shelter in the woods and he had written "INVESTIGATE FURTHER" under the date.

Chrissy was so confused, and when she saw what the girls were looking at, her confusion grew by leaps and bounds.

In the box lay four bright blue stones and a beautiful red velvet bag. The velvet bag had beads all over it, and there was a large moonstone on the front of it.

She had to look twice when she realized the stones had a faint blue glow to them. Then she questioned her eyesight when they grew more vibrant every time she put her hands close. That in itself was strange but what was even stranger was how the stones started vibrating with movement. It only happened when she put her hands directly over them. It was almost like they were drawn to her hands. A chill traveled down her spine, and she was ready to leave the attic.

"Girls! Let's get away from the box. Now." Both girls heard the urgency in the tone of her voice, and they scrambled to get up.

Now to figure out what to do with this stuff. In the end, Chrissy put the stones and the velvet bag back in the velvet box, and she put the velvet box and the gun back in her not-so-secret hiding place. She decided to take the tin box with the new contents back to their room.

"Oh, Uncle James," she said mostly to herself, "what in the world were you involved in?"

CHAPTER 9

Ronald Burgess was meeting with the Chief of Police and his Secretary when he felt a brief trickle in his blood. He knew the minute that someone had found and briefly activated at least one of the missing Stones.

Four of the Stones had vanished off the face of the earth many years before, and no one seemed to know where they were. *Who could have them?*

He had been searching for the missing Stones for over a hundred years, and, up until today, he had not been able to sense them anywhere.

After not finding them for so long, he figured they were buried somewhere. Which was a good thing. He wanted them destroyed, after all. But they couldn't be destroyed. He had tried and tried to do away with the two he had, to no avail.

He glanced over at his bookcase to make sure the two he had hiding in plain sight were still there. Yep. Still sitting on top of a couple of different books.

Why were the missing ones here? Why now? He wondered if whoever had them knew what they were.

He gritted his teeth to keep from screaming at the Police Chief, who wouldn't stop talking. The Chief had no idea what was at stake. He was a mere human with nothing special about him.

Ronald knew that everything could be ruined if The Stones were fully activated and used. He felt anger hit him hard at the thought of all his plans falling apart. Everything he had worked for. Years and years of sacrifices. Years and years of starting over and growing old. The Stones held the key to his ruin.

He was prepared to do whatever it took to end the cycle he had endured the past 200 years. He was almost where he needed to be. He only had a couple of months and a few more sacrifices.

He knew from experience that he would do anything to make the cycle come to an end. His actions over the years had shown that he would do just that. Whatever it took. No matter who got in the way, he would eliminate them. His wife, his children, nothing was more important than ending the cycle and claiming his immortality. It was, after all, for the greater good.

Ronald reminded himself that the people needed a leader who had their best interest at heart. A leader who would be willing to make the required sacrifices for the desired end results. That leader was him. It had to be. Why else would he have been the one to find The Stones all those years ago? Why else would The Ancient One have chosen to communicate with him over everyone else?

The thought of all his work and sacrifice over the years being for nothing caused anger to consume him. He could not control himself as he yelled, "GET OUT!" to the people in the room with him.

The Police Chief looked up at him with a stunned expression, but his Secretary didn't even blink. She had witnessed his outbursts many times before. What she didn't know was that he was past the outburst phase. He was going to start killing people if they didn't get out of his presence.

"I SAID GET OUT! NOW!!!" He screamed as he started slinging stuff off the conference room table.

They both got up and walked out but not before he saw his Secretary roll her eyes. Who did she think she was?!? He couldn't believe she would dare to make fun of him. HOW DARE HER!!!

The only thing that helped him regain his composure was the glee he felt at his decision to make her the first person he would take for the upcoming sacrifice. He would be making a late-night visit to his Secretary, and he absolutely could not wait.

CHAPTER 10

After dinner, Chrissy put the girls to bed, curled up in the recliner, and opened the letter her Uncle James had left in her tin box.

My dearest Chrissy,

Oh, my dear girl. Where shall I begin? This is not a letter I am looking forward to writing. Therefore, it is probably best that I simply tell you with no further procrastination.

I have been researching my mother's and brother's deaths, and I believe that their deaths are connected. More specifically, I think that the same group of people murdered both. A dangerous group of people. A group of people who are full of evil.

Things are happening in Moon Lake that don't make sense. It's almost like something supernatural is here. Things aren't always what they seem, and I know this now more than ever.

These very things I have uncovered must have cost me my life. Even so, I have no regrets. I have lived my life knowing something was wrong in my life. That is why I never married. I couldn't bear the thought of possibly bringing children into Moon Lake. But I could not leave this place. I have always felt a strong connection to this town, even with everything that has happened here.

I plan on calling my friend Henry Kesselberg this week and asking him to come here. I need help. I need someone familiar with things that are not what they seem to be.

He may already be here in Moon Lake, living in his cabin on our property, and I hope that is the case. If not, please contact him in Los Angeles at 555-897-1377. Ask him to come as quickly as possible.

You can trust Henry with your life. He is a good man and will help you in any way possible. You can also trust Rose and Geoffrey. There is more to these people than meets the eye, but they will help you.

I am not sure what the Stones in the blue box do, but I sensed that they were important when I found them. Our family has an old cabin on our property that I had forgotten about. After I found new evidence, I found them there in the fallout shelter directly under the cabin.

Please don't do anything that will cause you to get hurt. The people involved in this are dangerous and will not think twice about hurting you or your girls.

Discuss things with Henry and trust him to take care of them. He is like no other person I ever met, and I pray you will lean on him during this time. He has secrets that I am sure he will share with you in time if you are around him long enough. I pray you will not hold anything he tells you against him.

Please watch the VHS tape as soon as possible. I won't tell you what is on it as you should see it yourself. The tape had been misplaced for over ten years, and I am so sorry. It was found after the kitchen faucet had a leak and caused us to replace the cabinets. The tape was wedged between the stove and a cabinet. It must have got-

ten knocked off the counter. Please forgive me for not contacting you sooner regarding the tape.

If you do decide to stay in Moon Lake, please trust your instincts and stay safe. Don't do anything without Henry being involved. I beg of you.

I love you,
Uncle James

P.S. You are, always have been, and always will be my niece. Never think otherwise. I love you and your girls more than words could ever express.

Chrissy was shocked at what she read in the letter. This doesn't make sense, she thought. However, nothing in her life had ever entirely made sense. She had just trusted that things were the way they were supposed to be. Was there some evil plan in place here? Even thinking that sounded crazy.

But could this be true? Had her daddy been murdered because of something that had to do with her grandmother's death? What about her mother? Had she been kidnapped and killed because of her grandmother's death as well? Her grandmother had died before Chrissy was born, way before her father and mother were even married. Could the people or person who killed her grandmother even still be alive? It was doubtful.

And what exactly did he mean by "you are, always have been and always will be my niece..."? Chrissy felt a headache coming on as a memory tickled at the back of her mind, and she grew frustrated when she couldn't quite place it. All she knew was there was water involved. She tried her hardest to force the memory to come to her mind, but she couldn't.

Chrissy's mind was going all over the place. None of this made sense!

Then her mind turned to what her Uncle James had written about Henry. She knew he had secrets, and she planned on finding out exactly what those secrets were. And what could he be talking about with Rose and Geoffrey? They weren't hiding anything. She was sure of that much.

She thought of the VHS tape and decided she needed to find a VCR right away. From what she had read in her letter, she knew there were more clues on the tape. And he had asked for her forgiveness regarding the video. She was very curious and knew there had to be a VCR in the main room. Surely.

She would watch the tape while the girls were sleeping and then investigate some of the information on those papers in her tin box. Thankfully the room she was in had double doors; she decided to leave the bedroom doors open if one or both girls woke up.

Satisfied that she had a plan, she left the bedroom and headed first to the kitchen to make a cup of hot cocoa before going to the main room to watch the tape and start her research.

She made her way to the main room and found Geoffrey and Rose watching *Nash Bridges.* At least there was a VCR she could use later.

After contemplating what to do, she decided she would start researching the papers full of names until Geoffrey and Rose decided to go to bed.

CHAPTER 11

Henry decided to do some research into the names on the list he had found in the basement. He stepped into the library and wasn't surprised to find Chrissy there already on the computer.

Whatever she was looking at had fully captured her attention. Henry took a moment to take in her beauty before alerting her to his presence. Believing he would never be able to share his feelings with Chrissy, he felt a sadness hit him right in his gut.

Pushing it aside, he cleared his throat so he wouldn't scare her. "Sorry. I was just planning on doing some research on the computer tonight, but I can come back when you're finished."

Chrissy swiveled around in the chair and felt the unwelcome butterflies stirring in her belly with the sight of Henry standing there.

"No need." She replied. "I don't know that I have the mental energy to go through this list tonight."

"List?" Henry asked. He kept a straight face even though his mind was going a hundred miles an hour.

"Well, it's the strangest thing. I found a list of names with dates of disappearances that Uncle James left behind."

"That is interesting," Henry continued, "I also have a list I found with names and dates of disappearances. It was in the basement, and I thought it might be important. It looks like we are on the same page as that is what I planned on researching."

"You may as well pull up a chair then, Henry. Let's compare our lists and see what we can come up with." Chrissy felt her energy spike after hearing that Henry also had a list and figured it would be better to work together. "Do you have any idea why Uncle James would have two lists about missing people?"

"It seems that James suspected something out of place here in Moon Lake, and he was looking into it."

"Did Uncle James tell you any specific details about what he suspected is or was going on here? And remind me how you and he knew one another?" Chrissy was itching to ask Henry what he was hiding but knew that would only alienate him.

"Chrissy, I will say that your Uncle was very concerned, and after what happened to him, you may want to walk away from this."

"Look, I know you may mean well, but whatever happened that you're talking about me walking away from happened to my family. I can't simply walk away without answers. Now, I'll ask again, did Uncle James give you any specific details about his suspicions?"

Henry should have known James's niece would be a little spitfire. Against his better judgment, he decided to share what he knew. "I will tell you what he shared, but you aren't going to like it. You will probably think it's crazy." He paused and raised an eyebrow, almost asking her permission to continue.

"Don't leave me hanging. You may as well tell me everything you know."

"He told me there is something evil here. He had come to believe there is a cult in Moon Lake and that his mother was somehow connected. James believes they had her killed when James and your father were children. He used the term "sacrificed." He had asked me to come the last time we spoke, and by the time I made it here the following night, it was already too late. I should have come sooner. If only I had, maybe he would still be alive." Henry sighed as he felt the regret from not coming quicker.

"Henry, if you knew Uncle James as well as I think you did, you know that he would not want you to take responsibility for this. It sounds like he knew that what he was looking into was dangerous."

"Why don't we work together to figure out what is going on? Once we figure it out, you can take your girls somewhere safe away from all this." Henry suggested.

"I am not saying I believe this, but let's pretend I do for now. If this is all true, then I think your plan would be our best and safest bet. My only concern is keeping my girls safe and as far away from danger as possible. Part of me wants to go back to Iowa, so I know they are safe, but the other part thinks that now that I have been here and know something is going on, we wouldn't be safe anywhere."

"Why don't we do some research tonight, and if we find out there's a real danger to your girls, you will take them home. With a bodyguard." When he saw that she was about to protest, he added, "At least for a few weeks."

"Agreed." Chrissy agreed that was a good plan. She wouldn't let her pride get in the way of her girls' safety. "Oh, and don't think I didn't notice how you evaded my questions about how you and Uncle James got to be so close, but I'll let you off the hook for now."

Henry wasn't sure if she was joking or not, so he chose not to reply.

After agreeing on the best route, they quickly discovered that the list Henry had found was a copy of Chrissy's original list with a decision made. So, there was no new information to add to either list.

They spent the next hour searching names and adding anything new to the list James had left them. There wasn't a lot more to add, but Henry kept seeing the same name. Bradley

Whitmore. What he found strange was that this man was linked to many disappearances. Before and after James's mother was murdered. So how was his name linked to a disappearance from the early 1900s and to one from 1970? He was cited as a witness. Could it be his grandfather with the same name? Or was Bradley Whitmore an immortal?

He called the fact that the man's name kept coming up to Chrissy's attention, and they started a detailed search of Bradley Whitmore. They located several articles that he was in, and his picture was the same in 1939 as it was in 1979. "How is this possible?" Henry asked.

Chrissy answered with another question, "What explanation could there be? And why are there so few articles on the missing people?"

They had found little to no information other than the missing person suspected of having fallen off the dam as one of their shoes was found near the dam or maybe a jacket or some other personal belonging. Other articles had wild animal attacks listed as the reason the person went missing.

"And why do all these articles sound the same?" Henry continued with their line of questions.

"And who exactly is Bradley Whitmore, and how is he connected to my family?"

"I don't know, but that is something we need to find out. How about we visit Bradley Whitmore tomorrow?"

"I think that would be a good place to start." Chrissy agreed they should investigate that man.

They spent another 30 minutes making notes and trying to make sense of the lists. Chrissy took a break to peek in on the girls, and they were both sound asleep.

As Chrissy was walking back to the office, she heard Bradley Whitmore's name coming from the main room. She stuck her head in the office and asked Henry to follow her.

Geoffrey and Rose were watching the Ten o'clock news,

and the news anchor was reading a headline, "Police are look-ing into the murder of Bradley Whitmore, who was found in his home this afternoon by his housekeeper. He had been tortured and killed. If you have any information, please contact the Moon Lake Police Department at...."

After it was over, they made their way back to the office. "What exactly is going on here, Henry? Could it be that whoever killed this man killed my Uncle James and is connected to the deaths of my father and grandmother?"

"I don't know, Chrissy, but I promise you I will help you get to the bottom of this." Henry made this promise, and he would keep it no matter what it cost him personally.

CHAPTER 12

"Geoffrey, I think we need to tell Henry and Chrissy what we know about The Council. I know you don't remember who we are exactly dealing with, honey, but we could at least tell them what you do remember." Rose whispered. She knew they were alone in their room but still wanted to be careful that no one heard them.

"Rose, I am afraid that would put them in even more danger. If they try to take on The Council Members, they will most certainly be killed. Plus, they may not even believe us. It does sound farfetched. I just wish I could remember all the details of my past. If only I could at least remember who the Council Members are." Geoffrey whispered back, trying his best to match her calm tone. "The best we can do for now is be here for them and guide them through this when we can. We can also pray that we find someone who can use The Stones."

"Even though we don't know who we are dealing with, we can't let The Council Members harm those precious girls. Promise me that you will consider telling them what you know if it comes down to it. Please, honey. For James. For me." Rose knew how to get to Geoffrey.

"If it comes down to it, yes, I will tell them everything I can remember. I promise I will not allow those girls to be harmed. My powers are gone, but I will protect them with my life."

Rose leaned over and placed a kiss on his cheek. "Thank you, honey. You are the best thing that ever happened to me."

"And you are the best thing that ever happened to me." He said as he kissed her back. He meant that with all his heart. Without Rose, he was not sure where he would be. Nowhere good, that is for sure.

He let his mind go back to that cold night a little over forty-five years earlier.

"Geoffrey, it is time for you to go on your first mission. You must prove your worth to the spirit inside you." A faceless man looked at him and knew there would be no arguments. This man was used to getting his way. "Your first sacrifice will be Rose Hallaway. See my second in command for your instructions and have her here by midnight. We must have time to prepare the body. The sacrifice will be for nothing if the body has not been properly purified."

The faceless man didn't know that Geoffrey would not ever be able to sacrifice Rose or anyone else. He had a love for people that Ronald would never understand.

Geoffrey had gotten ready like everything was in order and left the Community a little before eleven o'clock. He made it to Rose's home and snuck into her bedroom. Geoffrey and Rose locked eyes, and he felt an instant love that shook him to the core of his being. He had always loved people in general, but this was new to him.

Geoffrey had felt the spirit trying to gain control over his emotions. To force the love he felt for Rose out of his body, but Geoffrey fought with everything he had. The utter shock he felt when he felt the spirit leaving his body was still burned in his brain. He had a battle of wills with the spirit and had won!

He made a snap decision to kidnap her and start over in another state. They hadn't made it far before she confided in Geoffrey that her dad had worked for the faceless man and knew what was happening. She had been utterly shocked when she had overheard him agree to it. He was planning on sacrificing his only daughter so he could be part of some secret group in Moon Lake. Rose had been terrified and thought she would be dead before the week was out. She had wanted to escape but wasn't sure how with her father watching her like a hawk.

After spending a few weeks on the run, they knew they were in love. They got married and lived in a small house in Utah for a couple of years. George worked on a ranch, and Rose cooked meals for the ranch owners. Things were going well until Rose got homesick to see her mama.

They ended up reaching out to the only person Geoffrey trusted – Matt Kensington. Matt offered to cast a spell to cause people to think Geoffrey and Rose died so they could return to Moon Lake.

Geoffrey and Rose both agreed, and they moved home, living and working for Matt at The Lodge. The spell ensured no one would ever be able to remember them unless they knew what they were looking for. This had allowed Rose to see her Mother without being in danger. They had been living here for all this time without The Council knowing. They had kept their mouths shut, and so far, they had been safe.

Geoffrey wasn't sure why he couldn't remember names and faces unless someone had also put a spell on him when he left. He was very confused when it came to the details. He knew there was something terrible going on but couldn't remember everything it entailed. Who was the group? Why were they sacrificing people? Or was it all a dream? NO. He had to remember. He had to break free of the fog that was overtaking his memories. He had a feeling his memories held the key to keeping all those he cared about safe. Then it hit him. A face. A name.

Geoffrey set straight up in bed and grabbed Rose's arm. "Ronald Burgess. He's one of them. I remember him being a part of some group we were in."

"The MAYOR?!? That Ronald Burgess???"

"Yes. Ronald Burgess was there. I remember him specifically giving me an order to bring you back to this place where we were. It was cold, and I remember it was wet, but that's all I can remember."

"What are we going to do, Geoffrey? Do we take him on? Confront him?"

"Not right away. We first need to figure out what exactly The Council's endgame is."

"How are we going to do that?"

"It's vital I regain my memory. To do that, I need to go back to where I came from. Back to the beginning and put an end to whatever is happening."

CHAPTER 13

C hrissy filled Henry in on everything her Uncle James had written (well, almost everything) while they waited on Geoffrey and Rose to go to bed. As soon as the two left the main room, they headed straight to the VCR to watch the tape.

After Henry got the VCR fired up and the tape was inserted, they settled in on the leather sofa to see what was on the video.

A woman appeared on the screen, and Chrissy gasped and grabbed his arm, "Henry, that's my mother!"

Jocelyn Kensington started speaking, "Hello, James. If you are watching this, that means I am dead. Please hear me out and keep an open mind. You know that I never believed that wild animals attacked Allen. Nothing has ever been able to make me believe that, so I have spent the last five years investigating his death. What I found leads me to believe something is going on in Moon Lake. Something sinister. Something evil. Something that is connected to not only Allen's death but also Barbara's."

Henry looked over at Chrissy, and she had gone stark white. "Hey," he said softly, "are you ok?"

She just shook her head and kept watching, tears streaking her face. She still had his arm in her grasp, and he briefly considered holding her hand to offer comfort but decided against it. They weren't on that level yet, he thought.

He focused his attention back on the screen, "James, at least five, sometimes ten or more people have been disappearing from Moon Lake every year for at least the last fifty years. I have found that the same people are connected to these disappearances over and over. One man specifically is connected. His name is Bradley Whitmore. He has been involved in some capacity with over ten disappearances over thirty years. Maybe even longer."

Chrissy paused the tape and wept into her hands. Henry felt his heart squeeze with her sadness. He could feel it, and it hurt him like it was his own. He handed her a tissue, and she half-smiled in thanks. Then, after what seemed like minutes, Chrissy pulled herself together and started the tape playing.

Jocelyn started speaking again. "I know that shouldn't be possible, but it is true. Look into the names I have, and you will uncover the same thing. I have spent a lot of time researching the people who disappeared along with the people who are connected, and none of it makes any sense. It's like someone is behind the scenes making people believe all these disappearances are caused by animal attacks and people falling off the dam. I have come to believe it is all a lie – a big cover-up. I placed a copy of my research in a special cabin out in the woods. Think about it and you will know where to look. Think about where we used to play as kids, and you will know where to look. Please get it and figure out what is going on. And keep Chrissy out of this. Please. I want her to be safe, and if she gets involved, she won't be. And James, be careful. Please tell Chrissy I love her and that I'm sorry."

The video ended, and Chrissy looked over at Henry. "What am I supposed to do? I can't leave Moon Lake now. My mom was investigating my dad's murder, and it got her, and possibly Uncle James killed. I must bring their killers to justice. I'm going to the police first thing in the morning."

"Agreed on bringing the killers to justice, but not so sure you and your girls need to stay here and definitely not sure about going to the police." Henry wanted to honor not only James's wishes but also her mother's.

"I would at least like to continue our research a couple of weeks. If we find something sinister really is happening and I need to go, I will take my girls back home. And why shouldn't we get the police involved?"

"Your Uncle James didn't get them involved, and that is good enough reason for me. As far as staying a couple of weeks, that sounds like a good compromise. Let's continue with our research on the missing people in the morning. Maybe we can find a connection that will point us in the right direction."

"That sounds like a plan. Let's get some rest and meet back up in the morning. Have a good night, Henry. Thanks for everything."

"Good night, Chrissy."

Henry made his way back to the main room and settled back in on the couch. There was no way he would be leaving The Lodge that night. He wouldn't feel right leaving Chrissy and her girls alone.

Chrissy woke up at six o'clock the following morning, ready to spend the day looking for the fallout shelter, doing further research on the missing people, and then building out a timeline. An hour later, she walked into the main room with her second cup of coffee and a Sausage and Biscuit. "Good morning, Henry." She felt herself flush a little upon seeing him again.

"Morning, Chrissy." Wow. She looked gorgeous with her flushed cheeks, and even the sweatpants and shirt she was wearing worked in her favor.

"I want to watch the tape again. See if we missed anything important."

Henry mentally scolded himself for focusing on anything

other than their current situation and moved over to the VCR to get it powered up.

After the tape was over, they sat in silence for a few minutes letting everything soak in.

"I do need to show you something the girls and I found. I just need to get the girls their breakfast." Chrissy decided she would show Henry the glowing Stones and see if he could make sense of them.

A few minutes later, the girls were settled in the dining room for breakfast with Rose, and Chrissy and Henry were on their way to the attic.

"Keep in mind that this is my secret hiding spot, so you are part of the secret club now." Chrissy tried to keep the situation light. She tended to do that anytime she was upset or nervous.

"Well, I feel special," Henry replied with a wink. He smiled when he saw her cheeks turning an even darker shade of red.

"You should," Chrissy said with a smile, and then she walked to her secret spot and opened it up. She pulled the blue velvet box open and showed Henry the stones lying on top of the velvet pouch. "Henry, I have no idea what these are."

After she opened the box, he wasn't sure what to say. They were just blue stones. That is until she put her hand near them. *Whoa*, he thought. *The stones are glowing! Wait – are they moving?!?*

"Chrissy - How are you making them glow and vibrate?"

"I am not sure. I found the stones hidden here with the letter from Uncle James I told you about. The stones were in the box with a few other things he left for me to find, so they must be significant. Uncle James said he found them on our land in an old fallout shelter in the woods."

"Wow." He wasn't sure what to say.

"I plan on hiking out today to find the old cabin he said the fallout shelter was under. Do you want to go with me to find it?"

"Yes, I will go with you. There is no way you need to go alone."

CHAPTER 14

Rose had overheard some of what Chrissy and Henry discussed, so she volunteered to watch the girls. She said she would take them to lunch and to play at the park in town. Chrissy gladly accepted, and she and Henry were on their way to the woods a short time later.

Rose could tell how protective of her girls Chrissy was, so she had assured Chrissy she would keep them away from the dam outside of town. She knew how dangerous it was and didn't want to put the girls in harm's way.

Rose was thrilled to spend time with the girls. She and Geoffrey had not had children of their own, and they had loved spending time with Chrissy when she was little. So, Lela and Jessica were as close as they would ever get to grandkids, and she treasured time with them.

Henry suggested that he should drive, and Chrissy was perfectly fine with that. Especially since her palms were wet from sweat. She felt her nerves on edge but knew she had to stay strong. How many times had she had to tell herself that over the years? More times than she could count.

This would be the first time she had been in those woods since her daddy's body was found. She knew it wouldn't be easy, but it couldn't be avoided. She owed it to her family to figure out what happened and why.

Henry glanced over at Chrissy as they were getting in his

Jeep, "How are you holding up?"

"Honestly, I was just giving myself a pep talk. Reminding myself, I must stay strong to get to the bottom of what happened to my parents, uncle, and even those who have disappeared over the years. They also need justice."

She paused before continuing. "Henry, you don't have to stay here and get yourself any more mixed up in this than you already are. I won't blame you if you decide to bow out of this situation and go back home to Los Angeles. This isn't your fight, and I would hate for you to get hurt."

"I appreciate your concern, but I know what I am doing. James was my closest friend, and I owe it to him to finish what he started. He would want me to stay here and help you. Believe me when I say I wouldn't be able to live with myself if I left and something happened to you or your girls." Henry knew he couldn't leave her and hoped she would understand.

"You never did tell me how you are related to Uncle James' old friend, Henry. Was he your dad? Is that how you and Uncle James got to know one another?"

Henry wasn't prepared for these questions. He knew he should have been, but he hadn't allowed himself to get close to many people over the years. So, not a lot of questions had been asked. Still, he knew he had to answer.

"Chrissy, that is a very long story. Is it one we can talk about later? I don't want to get into it and get interrupted. Would that be ok with you?" He felt like a chicken. But he didn't know how she would react if he told her his story right now... *"Oh, yeah, I am an immortal...yeah, my mom turned me into one after I was shot a hundred or so years ago..." Ummm, no*, he thought. *She would probably freak out and ban me from the lodge. Better to stall her. Better to wait until they knew each other better. There was no telling what her reaction would be.*

"Yes, that would be fine. I don't mean to get into your business. Sometimes I am way too nosy." Chrissy knew he had some secrets of his own, but she would wait and deal with his secrets after they got to the bottom of the current mystery of Moon Lake. She had trusted her Uncle James with her life and knew he would never tell her she could trust Henry if she couldn't. He would never put her and the girls in harm's way.

CHAPTER 15

R onald Burgess stood in his office window watching an older woman and two little girls walk down the sidewalk. He knew the woman, but he just couldn't place her. He had to know her from somewhere because she looked so familiar.

He watched them until they disappeared into the Country Café. Then, after telling his temporary secretary to cancel his one o'clock meeting with the Sheriff, he made the split decision to have lunch at the Country Café.

A few minutes later, he spoke to the waitress and took a few minutes to say hello to the customers who were dining in. Doing that made it seem natural to walk up to the table with the woman and two kids.

Rose, Lela, and Jessica had just settled into a booth and were about to order when she felt a chill travel down the back of her spine. She knew there was an evil presence in the Café. Even though she didn't have any powers, she could still feel it.

Not wanting to cause a scene by jumping up and taking the girls out of there as quickly as possible, she kept her composure and ordered burgers and fries for the girls and the lunch special, meatloaf, mashed potatoes, green beans, and a roll for herself. The girls had asked her if they could have a small ice cream cone for dessert if they ordered water with their meal, and she had agreed before she knew that "man" would be coming to the café.

She could feel him staring at them. So, she wasn't surprised when he approached their booth. "Hello and welcome to Moon Lake. I don't recognize you two young ladies as locals, so you must be here visiting. I'm Ronald Burgess, the Mayor of Moon Lake, and I couldn't leave without saying hi and giving you an official welcome!" He said this with such enthusiasm he could almost be in a commercial teaching people how to be welcoming and friendly. HA, Rose thought to herself, he is up to something.

"Hi, I'm Jessica, and this is my sissy Lela. Her real name is Louise, but we call her Lela. We are visiting with our mama, and this is Ms. Rose. She makes the best pancakes in the world!"

"Nice to meet you, three ladies. Are you all staying at The Lodge?"

Before Rose could hush her, Jessica answered, "We are! Our Uncle James got sick, and he passed away, and now mama is his hair."

Lela corrected her, "You mean his HEIR, Jessi, not his HAIR!"

"That is so nice. I must be going now. Enjoy your stay in Moon Lake." Ronald was barely able to contain the emotional outburst close to boiling over before he could get back to his office.

Ronald stepped up to his temporary secretary and told her he would be out of pocket for the rest of the day. He was happy that she showed him the respect he deserved when she said, "Yes, sir. Please let me know if I can do anything for you." He thought she was much more pleasant than his previous secretary. No matter, his old secretary and her holier than thou self would get what was coming to her soon enough.

He could still picture the sheer terror on the old hag's face when he woke her from a deep sleep. Even better was thinking back to the moment he held her at gunpoint and made her leave her home with him. He marched her to his car and made her get in the trunk.

The look on her face told him she thought he was going to kill her. She was right, of course. But he wasn't going to kill her right away. That would come the following month, so she had a little time left to live. Memories like that made him happy.

He knew he would soon be done with the cycles of aging, and he could not wait. And now that he had two more ultimate sacrifices, he would be able to live as his young self for a very long time. Becoming an immortal and living forever with his bride was his end goal.

He let his mind wander to his future bride. Sweet, sweet Jocelyn. He had loved her from the moment he laid eyes on her but was not able to do anything about it until her husband died. It was no matter to him that her husband happened to be his grandson. Nobody even remembered that little tidbit of information. The yearly spell he cast over Moon Lake had caused people to forget who he was over and over and over again.

It was unfortunate that Jocelyn had been married to Barbara Jean's son. But he couldn't let his sentiments over Barbara Jean get in the way of his eternal happiness.

He thought back to his late daughter, Barbara Jean, and how he still missed her smiling face. She had been a daddy's girl after she had lost her mom, Patricia, to cancer. At least she thought that's what happened to her mom. Ronald had sacrificed Patricia when Barbara Jean was in the ninth grade. He had wanted to wait until Barbara Jean was married, but The Ancient One had been anxious, so he had complied.

Barbara Jean had ended up getting married and having her own family at a young age. Even though Ronald hadn't agreed with her choice for a husband, Ronald was proud of himself for allowing her that time. He had given her several years of happy times before he took her.

That one had indeed hurt him, but he had to do it. He didn't get to choose which family members he sacrificed; that was up to The Ancient One.

He remembered how furious Matt Kensington had been after he found out Ronald had given the order to sacrifice Barbara Jean while Matt was out of town buying supplies for his Lodge. Ronald had told Matt not to marry Barbara Jean, but he wouldn't listen. Stupid fool!

Matt had thought he could stay married to Barbara Jean until she died of natural causes. He should have known better! Then he thought he would be allowed to raise their two boys, Allen and James, without consequences. Wrong, again.

They were a family in mourning for their lost wife and mother one day, then the next, Allen and James forgot their father had been there at all. They had memories of their father running off and leaving them after their mother died. They thought he just couldn't bear the grief of losing his wife. They had forgiven him and lived without regret for the rest of their days. Allen was old enough to take guardianship of James, and they were able to keep the Lodge going. Ronald felt like he had been generous to his grandsons by giving them those times and those memories.

He had given the job of Barbara Jean's sacrifice to Bradley Whitmore and had only recently found out that the fool allowed Allen and James to be there when she was thrown into the pit. After Barbara Jean was sacrificed, Ronald had erased himself from their memories. He couldn't bear to be around Barbara Jean's boys. It had simply hurt too much.

CHAPTER 16

C hrissy and Henry made their way through the wooded areas as quickly as they could. Only stopping to rest when they were tired of hiking. Or at least when Chrissy was tired of hiking. They both had a feeling that time was of the essence but couldn't put their finger on the exact reason why.

After almost two hours of hiking, resting, and walking, they came upon an old, abandoned cabin and decided that it had to be the one. Chrissy watched as Henry looked in the front window before trying the front door. Luckily, the door was not locked. "I will walk in and make sure it's safe before you come in." He said to Chrissy.

Chrissy nodded and walked over to the window so she could watch. Henry walked around the cabin, and she saw him pull on a lever on the floor before walking back towards her. He opened the cabin door and motioned for her to follow him.

Henry pulled the lever and found that it opened a secret passage going down to a basement. He shined his flashlight down into the cellar, "Let me go down the stairs before you head down. I want to make sure they are all solid and will hold our weight."

Once he reached the bottom, he yelled for her to come down the stairs and be careful. She started making her way down the stairs and was touched to see Henry waiting with his hand out, ready to help her down. She felt her traitorous heart beating way too fast, and her face was getting hot again, and she had never been more thankful for a dimly lit area in her life. She would be mortified if Henry saw her red face.

Henry felt Chrissy's heartbeat kick up a notch, and it made him happy. He liked the fact that she found him attractive because he had already developed feelings for her. He wasn't sure how he allowed that to happen, but he had. Although, he could never let her know he felt anything for her. Their lives were too different. She was a human, and he was not.

He looked at Chrissy and found her staring at him with an odd expression on her face. "You alright?"

"I am. Just thinking." She felt like screaming with joy when they realized the stairs led to the old fallout shelter. This was the cabin!

After spending a few minutes looking around, they decided there wasn't much to find in the fallout shelter. So they made their way back up to the cabin to continue their search.

Chrissy looked around and felt such a connection to the cabin. It was old and rustic. It had such beauty, and she would love to rehab it and bring it back to its previous glory.

Wait. She owned the cabin, she told herself. It was on her land. She could do it! She could do it! She quickly scolded herself for thinking of such things when she needed to be focused on more severe issues.

Chrissy walked over to the old fireplace and started searching it. She filled Henry in, "I am going to start with searching this fireplace. I am not sure why, but I am drawn to it."

"Let's start with the chimney and move around the perimeter of the room."

Chrissy found a loose brick in the chimney. "Henry, I found something!"

He came over to the fireplace as she pulled out a wad of money. "What!" she said before opening the cash and finding a letter wrapped up inside it.

Meanwhile, Henry had found another loose brick that held old photographs from what looked like the mid to late 1800s to the early 1900s.

"Chrissy, this is an amazing find. I vote that we finish our search quickly and take this all back to The Lodge to go through it. We can return it here after we uncover everything we can about who hid it here. Or we can leave it here. Whichever you feel comfortable with will be fine with me."

Chrissy agreed with Henry, and they made their way out of the cabin and started the hike to Henry's Jeep.

"Henry, what do you think is going on here?" Chrissy broke the silence.

"I wish I had the answers for you, Chrissy. I truly do." If only she knew how much he wanted to get her the answers she needed. "Have you decided if you are going to stay here and run The Lodge, or will you be going back home once all this is over?"

Chrissy sighed, "I haven't decided as to what we will be doing after this is over. I have a business in Iowa that I have temporarily closed. I don't have any employees, so I was able to close it without any major issues."

"I hope you decide to stay." He couldn't help himself. He wanted Chrissy and the girls to stay so he could get to know them all better. To care for them. To provide for them.

Whoa, slow down. Henry mentally scolded himself for allowing those feelings to surface.

Chrissy didn't know how to respond to that just yet, so she busied herself by reading the letters they had found.

CHAPTER 17

Chrissy pulled out the first letter and started reading it out loud to Henry. It was dated March 26, 1921.

My Dearest Love Barbara Jean,

The moment I saw you, my mind was altered, and my heart was whole. I loved you then, and I love you even more now.

Imagine my joy, my complete and utter happiness when you said you love me, too. How can someone such as you ever love a man such as me?

I am not worthy of your love, yet I crave it. I am not worthy of you, yet I must have you.

My life now belongs to you, my dear. It is yours to do with as you will. Please say you will run away with me. Let us leave this place and start over somewhere far away.

Somewhere where there is no Council. Where there is no Ronald Burgess. Where there is no more need for sacrifice.

Please say you will. Meet me at our spot tonight with your answer. I am yours to do with as you please. If you find it too hard to leave Moon Lake, I will stay. As long as we are together, I can face anything.

Yours truly forever and always,

Matt

Chrissy was beet red after reading that letter out loud. She felt like she had violated Matt and Barbara Jean by reading the letter. It was so personal and heartfelt. *Matt and Barbara Jean? Her grandparents? Could it be? It had to be.*

Henry was the first to speak after she finished reading the letter. "I wonder what he meant by *'Somewhere where there is no Council, where there is no Ronald Burgess. Where there is no more need for sacrifice'.* That is an odd thing to put in a letter."

Chrissy nodded her head in agreement. "Doesn't make a lot of sense, that's for sure."

She picked up the pile of old pictures and was shocked at what she saw. "Henry, I recognize the people in this photo." She turned two different photos over and looked at the writing on the back. "This can't be possible."

She had piqued his curiosity, "Who is it?"

"Do you mind pulling over? I need you to look at these pictures and tell me I am seeing things or maybe even losing my mind."

Henry pulled over and looked at the photo Chrissy held. "This picture is of my grandparents, my Uncle James, and my daddy. It was taken in 1946. Look at the back of the picture. It says Matthew Robert Kensington, Wife Barbara Jean Burgess Kensington, Sons Allen DeWitt Kensington, three years old, and James Edward Kensington, one-year-old."

Then she moved on to the next picture. "This one is dated over a hundred years ago. Now, look at the back of this picture. It says Matthew Robert Kensington, Wife Margaret Anna Williams Kensington, Sons Matthew James Kensington, five years old, John Edward Kensington, three years old and daughter, Elizabeth Mary Kensington, one-year-old." She looked at him with a look that almost scared him.

"Henry, this is the same man. Look at him. Please tell me I

am mistaken." She almost begged. "I have to be mistaken."

Henry couldn't tell her any such thing. It was the same man. No doubt. The facial expression, the smile, the ears, the nose. Everything was identical. "Chrissy, I can't tell you that because I agree with you. The men look identical in both photos." Henry replied as softly as he could. "Why don't we get back to The Lodge and ask Geoffrey and Rose if they know anything about this man."

He eased the Jeep back onto the highway and headed to The Lodge. He had an uneasy feeling in his stomach. He didn't think this man and the other man named Bradley Whitmore were actual Immortals, but something was going on.

Maybe it was time to call his Mama.

CHAPTER 18

Jocelyn Kensington wiped the sweat from her brow with her towel and looked down at her rose bush. It had been in dire need of pruning, and she was irritated with herself for not doing it sooner. She finished clearing away the dead pieces before sitting on her bench with a glass of ice water. Her mind had been running away with itself due to a dream she'd had the night before.

In her dream, she held a baby girl in a nursery that was painted light pink and gray with animals all over the walls. The baby was hungry, so she had breastfed the baby in her dream. What struck her as odd in the dream was how she felt such an intense love when the baby girl looked up at her with her big, brown eyes.

Her dream continued with the baby suddenly disappearing out of her arms. She had jumped up and looked all around the room she was in, and she couldn't find the baby. That's when she woke up.

She woke up feeling a strong sense of despair. The love she felt for that baby in her dream was so strong that it almost seemed natural. The fear she felt when the baby disappeared also seemed real.

Jocelyn knew it couldn't be real as she didn't have any children. She had a young enough housekeeper to be her daughter, and they were close, but she wasn't her child.

She knew she couldn't focus on things that came to her in a dream. They weren't real. Maybe she simply wanted a child so severely that she was dreaming one up. That must be it!

A thought came to her that she would have to speak to her fiancé about. She wanted to adopt a child. Maybe they could do that after they were married! She knew it would be hard to adopt, but surely there was a child in need somewhere that they could help.

Just thinking about adopting had made her feel better, and she decided to speak to her fiance when he returned home.

Her fiance had done so much for their little community. She smiled, thinking about how he had continued to put others before himself time and again over the years. She was a lucky woman to have this man love her.

Several years earlier, the world had suffered several major earthquakes that had caused volcanoes worldwide to erupt. The catastrophes had changed life as everyone knew it. Millions had been killed, and those who had survived were in communities such as the one they lived in. It was difficult to travel, but her fiance and a few of the men were brave enough to go out in search parties, and most of the time, they would be gone for several weeks searching for those who were hurt or in need of help.

She was proud of him, not only for braving the world but primarily for how he found people who were in trouble and would bring them back to their community to take care of them. He was so giving and made an extra effort to ensure these people were welcomed into this community as their new home. It was almost like he made it his mission to make these lost people comfortable and happy.

He had recently brought a woman to their community captured by a small group of terrorists. Luckily for her, she had managed to escape and was hiding from them when her fiance spotted her. Sadly, they had beat her almost to death, but she was being well taken care of in their clinic. Thank goodness she was found before it was too late.

He had done that for her once. She had been lost, home-less, and on the brink of death when he found her in an old, abandoned cabin. He had brought her to this community and nursed her back to health. The two of them falling in love had been unexpected, but it almost seemed like their destiny.

He was a widower, and she had sensed a sadness about him, and for some reason, she had made it her mission to make him smile.

She couldn't remember much about her previous life other than deep loneliness after the great earthquake. However, she did faintly remember being married and losing her husband to the great earthquake, but his face had faded away over the years. She and her fiance had that in common, losing their mate, and they had brought one another comfort and love.

The face she saw for her future was Ronald's. Kind, loving Ronald.

CHAPTER 19

R onald Burgess carefully made his way down the trail until he reached the opening to the cave. He put his sweater on and eased down the ladder, landing on the concrete pathway. He walked for another ten minutes until he reached the wooden bridge over the flowing stream. He was thankful for having the bridge built a few months after they had discovered the cave. After crossing the bridge, he stopped to admire the waterfall. Looking at the waterfall was something he never had tired of.

It took him another five minutes of steady walking before he entered a doorway that led to their large meeting room just outside of the clearing used for sacrificing to The Ancient One.

Four men sat around a rock table the size of a car, and two more men stood off to the side against the wall. George Watkins jumped up when he saw Ronald and almost screamed, "What did you do to Bradley?!?!"

Knowing he had to maintain control not only of the Council Members but also the men standing by the wall, Ronald walked up to George and backhanded him, "Don't you EVER question me, or you will find out firsthand what I did to Bradley. Do you understand me, George?"

He then looked around at the men surrounding the table and landed on Lucas Rollings, "Would anyone else in the room like to continue this discussion, or is the matter closed?"

Ronald had no idea that Lucas was getting tired of Ronald's bullying. Lucas hadn't planned to take over The Council, but he was beginning to think he should entertain the idea.

One of the newer Council Members, Robert Vines, spoke up, "I say the matter is closed other than we are down another Council Member. That makes a total of three original Council Members we have lost, Ronald. Do you have another replacement in mind?" He glanced over at the men who were standing against the wall. They both looked hopeful but knew there were no guarantees that either of them would be picked to become a Council Member.

"I will handpick our replacement Council Member during our next meeting. Bring names, and I expect to see data to back up who you nominate." He made it a point to look each Council Member in their eyes. "Now that we have an understanding let's move on. Matt Kensington's granddaughter is in town for James's funeral. I found out today that she is the sole heir to the Kensington estate. Lucas, I want you to follow her around. Find out what her plans are and report back to me. I expect to be apprised of every move she makes."

"I will start tailing her first thing tomorrow morning." Lucas Rollings agreed.

"Good. Now, let's continue with the next topic. We need to gather our sacrifices and bring them to The Community by the end of next month. We have to ensure we will have what we need to complete the ultimate offering. On top of that, we need one per month for our monthly offering. I have two in mind for the ultimate offering. Who else has someone?"

Lucas had someone in mind, "There's a new woman named Sharon at the homeless shelter who came to us in the last couple of weeks. She was an only child, and her parents are both deceased, so she would be someone that would be easy to take. I doubt it would even get reported. Especially after I tell the Director that she told me she was planning on leaving us."

"Good, good. Lucas, you have been going above and beyond here lately. First, that traveling salesman and now the woman at the homeless shelter. This will be your second one this month, and your dedication has not gone unnoticed." Ronald said. "George, what about you? You plan on letting Lucas continue to outdo you?"

"I will have someone before the next meeting."

"See that you do. Anyone else?"

Both Robert Vines and Anthony Hightower also agreed to have someone before the next meeting. They moved on to the next topic of discussion, figuring out which of the Council Members would stay behind in the Community and who would be part of the "search party" going back to Moon Lake before the meeting was adjourned.

The mist clung to the wall, listening intently to Ronald Burgess speaking to the men in the room with him. He thought he was in control. He craved power and would do anything, sacrifice anyone to get it.

The mist felt such an intense hatred for the man it was almost convinced Ronald could feel the hate emanating from its body. The mist could feel what used to be hands itching to choke the life out of the man's miserable body. Some days the mist longed to walk around above in its human body, but days like today, it was glad to travel around without notice.

One day soon, it would have enough power to walk the earth in its human form. Enough power to create and then release more of its children on the planet. Ronald would be eliminated, and someone else would oversee the sacrifices. Someone who could be trusted.

The mist watched Ronald Burgess closely, hoping he could feel a presence. But he never turned around, never gave any indication he knew he was being watched. He never gave any indication that he knew his fate was sealed.

But he would know. One day soon.

CHAPTER 20

Henry and Chrissy went straight to the Dining Room when they got back to The Lodge. "Something smells delicious." Chrissy stated as they made their way to the table where Rose and the girls sat.

"Hello, you two." Rose greeted them as she got up and hugged them both. "I have a Chicken Casserole in the oven. It'll be ready in around 30 minutes."

"Mommy! Mommy! Ms. Rose let us have a small ice cream cone after lunch today!!!" Jessica could barely contain her excitement as she filled everyone in on their lunch and time at the park.

"We had water to drink with our burgers, Mommy, so an ice cream was ok." Lela made sure that her mommy knew they had been sensible for lunch.

Chrissy hugged both girls. "I take it my baby girls had a good time today, huh?"

Both girls nodded, and Jessica asked, "Mommy, can we play with our Barbie dolls for a little while?"

"Absolutely. Go on in the playroom, and I will come to get you when dinner is ready."

Geoffrey walked in as the girls were sprinting to the playroom, "Whoa, little ladies. Where's the fire?"

He chuckled, and Rose answered, "They are running off on

a vital mission… to play with their Barbie Dolls."

Chrissy turned to Geoffrey and Rose, "I appreciate you both for making me and my girls feel so comfortable and at home here."

Rose jumped up and hugged Chrissy again, "Honey, this *is* your home."

Henry looked around the table and wished he could freeze the moment. "Would you two be willing to meet with Chrissy and me in the morning about some mysteries we could use some help figuring out?"

Geoffrey looked over at Rose, "Of course, we are willing to help."

"We appreciate that. How does tomorrow right after breakfast sound?"

Geoffrey nodded. "That will be just fine."

During dinner, Rose decided to ask Chrissy about her plans, "Chrissy, have you thought about what you're going to do with The Lodge? If you decide to reopen, Geoffrey and I want you to know that we would love to stay on if you'll have us."

"Rose, I can't tell you how much that means to me, but I am still working through that."

Geoffrey added his thoughts, "Rose, honey, let's make sure Chrissy has all the facts before we get her to commit to any-thing."

Although Chrissy found what Geoffrey said odd, she de-cided it would be best to gather more information before asking what he meant by that statement.

Henry had known Geoffrey and Rose were hiding some-thing ever since he had met them, but he also felt that they meant no harm, so he hadn't ever engaged them about their past.

Geoffrey and Rose were both aware that Henry was an Immortal, but they had never said anything. They had known him for over twenty years, and he still looked the same as he did the day they met. When they figured it out, they had discussed it and decided to keep it to themselves.

All that was about to change: it had to, or they would not stand a chance against The Council.

George Watkins nervously checked his rearview mirror for the third time. He had to make sure no one was tailing him for the third time since heading to the payphone booth. He knew what he was risking but couldn't live with himself any longer. He had to warn Geoffrey Hamilton.

He had befriended Geoffrey around twenty years earlier and knew right away that there was something familiar about him. A few years into their friendship, he decided he would cast a spell of remembrance. That's when he knew who Geoffrey and Rose were. He had never shared his knowledge with another soul. Geoffrey's dad had been his closest friend, and he would keep quiet for his sake.

He knew things were about to change, and he couldn't continue allowing things to happen without trying to do something. Ronald was growing stronger day by day, and soon he would rule them all. Well, he and the evil spirit he worshipped.

George hated them all. Even the spirit living inside his own body. He hated it with a passion. He just hid it well. Over the years, he had figured out how to hide his mind from the spirit. He let it see what he wanted it to and nothing more.

George wanted out. It was time to end his own life. He would do it after helping Geoffrey and Rose.

CHAPTER 21

Rose jerked awake out of a dead sleep to the phone ringing.

"Who in the world would be calling at this hour?" Rose asked as Geoffrey climbed out of bed to answer the ringing phone.

"Thank you for calling The Lodge. This is Geoffrey speaking."

"Geoffrey, this is George Watkins. It is imperative we speak."

"George! We aren't supposed to meet until next week. What is so important that it couldn't wait?"

"I am not who you think I am. Geoffrey, do you remember anything at all about The Council?"

"What are you talking about?" Geoffrey was leery of telling George anything about what he had remembered. He wasn't sure why George was asking questions. Could he possibly be a Council Member? He thought George was the Postmaster. Oh no. Could he have been tricking him this whole time? Was their friendship a lie?

"Please listen to me! I understand that Matt Kensington's granddaughter is here in Moon Lake. You must warn her. The Council leader is planning something that he's not telling The Council, but I think it has to do with her." George warned.

Geoffrey decided to play along. He needed to know if Chrissy was in danger. "Tell me what you know."

"I know he has assigned another Council Member to follow her around, starting tomorrow. I am risking too much being here, but I owe it to Matt to do what I can to keep his granddaughter safe."

"How are you involved in this, and why are you telling me? Why do you owe anything to Matt Kensington?"

"We were friends. Matt and I. Along with your father. We were inseparable for years. Not to mention your father was my closest friend. That's what made you familiar to me. You look and act a lot like your father."

"You knew my father?"

"Geoffrey, I know you must remember something. I am telling you all this so you can be alert. There's so much more I need to share with you. One thing you must know, Ronald Burgess is the one who kidnapped Jocelyn Kensington all those years ago. She's living in The Community, and..."

"And what!?!" Geoffrey asked, almost harshly.

All Geoffrey heard in return was silence, then what sounded like a scraping sound before a different, all too familiar voice from his past was on the line.

"May I ask who this is?" Ronald Burgess politely asked.

Geoffrey quickly hung the phone up, his heart slamming in his chest. *Oh, no,* he thought. *Please let George be alright.*

Geoffrey walked back to the bedroom he shared with Rose and found her sound asleep. *Sweet dreams, my beautiful wife. The morning will come soon enough, and I will fill you in on what has transpired before breakfast. We can make plans to deal with the situation then.*

CHAPTER 22

After a hearty breakfast, the girls ran off to play in the garden while the adults sat down at the corner table in the Main Room.

"Don't leave the patio area. Y'all will have to come in if you get out of my sight." Chrissy said.

"Awe, mommmm. We're not babies." Jessica pouted.

Chrissy gave Jessica the eye. The look that let Jessica know she meant business. "You heard me. Stay where I can see you."

"Yes, ma'am." She pouted for another half a second before jumping up and running out the door – yelling at Lela. " I want to play BARBIES!"

Chrissy watched the girls as they settled in on the patio. Then she put a notebook, pen, the letter from her Uncle James, the photos, and the VHS tape on the table and looked over at Henry, queuing him to lead the conversation.

Henry could tell she didn't know where to start, so he began, "First of all, thank you both for agreeing to speak with us. We are hoping you can help us figure out why the man in these pictures appears to both be Matt Kensington."

Chrissy had tears in her eyes as she spoke up, "Please help us figure out what is happening in Moon Lake. My daddy, mama, and uncle were all killed due to something that happened with my grandma many years ago. My gut feeling tells me that none of them died of natural causes."

Geoffrey felt the guilt spread immediately with Henry's words thanking them, and it got even worst when Chrissy spoke. He sure didn't deserve any thanks.

He picked up the old photos, "Matt Kensington was a good friend of mine. He took me in when I was a young man and helped me sort out the life I had been born into. He especially helped me understand what it means to have a love for your fellow man. My father had been shot and killed when I was seven years old, and Matt was a father figure for me."

"Wait a minute," Chrissy interrupted. "Are you speaking of my great-grandfather? No offense, but my grandfather wouldn't have been old enough to be a father figure to you. He would have only been a few years older than you unless you are a lot younger than you look. No offense."

"None taken. If all things were as they seem, you would be correct," Geoffrey replied. "Please understand, things are happening that make no sense. I have very few memories of my past. Things have been coming back in bits and pieces, but not enough to make sense of everything in my past. At least not yet."

"I still don't understand how your past would include my grandfather being a father figure to you. Please elaborate."

"Something happened several years ago that caused me to forget a great deal about my past. Just recently, I have started remembering a few things from my past but not all things. However, I will tell you everything I do remember. My father, Arthur Hamilton, was somehow involved in a secret group with several other men. Powerful men. After he died, this group of men who call themselves The Council picked me to take his place."

"You don't remember these men?" Henry asked.

"Up until last night, I only remembered that they wanted me to help them harm Rose."

"Harm Rose?!?" Chrissy looked at Geoffrey then at Rose. "Why would they want to harm Rose? What happened?"

Rose spoke up. "My father had wanted to be a part of the "secret group" so badly that he offered me up to get his foot in the door. I remember very well what they planned for me. I heard it and was scared to death when my father agreed for me to be a sacrifice." She leaned over and grabbed a tissue off the coffee table to blow her nose.

"Sacrificed?" Chrissy felt her blood pressure rising.

Rose shook her head. "Being a part of the Council was more important than I ever was to my father."

Geoffrey didn't like seeing her hurt by recounting those difficult memories. "Honey, do you want to take a break?"

"I don't think time will allow me to take a break. Anyways, I overheard my father talking to a man one night when I was supposed to be sleeping. I remember being so confused as to why he would want to give me up for a group, and I had been trying to get up my nerve to run away. But my father was always watching. It's like he knew I would try to run away."

Rose smiled at Geoffrey with so much love on her face. "The night Geoffrey came, I thought I would be dead before the night was out. But, instead, he took me far away, and we ended up getting married a few short weeks later."

Henry couldn't believe what he had heard. "Wow. That is unbelievable. How did you end up back in Moon Lake?"

"Rose missed her mother, so after a couple of years, we decided to come home. I contacted your grandfather, Matt, and he helped us come home."

"What did he do?"

"First, you all need to understand that the men in the Council have certain powers. These powers, from what I remember, come from magic stones. Your grandfather used some of his power to cause people to not recognize Rose and me. This allowed us to move back home without fear of being found out. Anyone from our past with bad intentions can hear our names and even see our faces and still not recognize us. I left the Council and am better off for it. Living life with my Rose is worth more to me than a hundred lifetimes without her could ever be."

"What do you mean by living a hundred lifetimes without her?" Chrissy was curious about that statement.

Geoffrey had a strange expression on his face. "I can't rightly say what I meant by that. It just came out without me thinking."

"What do the Stones you talked about look like, and how many Stones are there?" Chrissy enquired of Geoffrey.

"I remember the men saying they had two of the six Stones. The one I saw was orangish or maybe even redder at first, but after they transferred the power to me, it turned a blue color."

"I have the other four." Chrissy blurted out.

"They are here?" Rose asked.

"Yes. Uncle James found them in an old cabin in the woods and hid them in one of the secret places I had when I was a kid. Want me to get them?"

"No. Leave them where they are. We will need the stones to stop these powerful men of The Council." Geoffrey warned.

"How will we use the Stones to stop the men? Do you remember?" Henry asked Geoffrey.

"Not exactly. I know that a descendant of the Quapaw Indians will need to be found, but I can't remember why or what the Indians have to do with everything. However, I do know that we need to find someone with Quapaw blood in their veins."

The blood drained from Chrissy's face. She felt like she was going to pass out. Her mind was racing almost out of control. *This can't be happening.*

Geoffrey rubbed his temples for a moment. Then he suddenly jumped up like he had been shot, "That's IT! We need to go to Oklahoma and meet with the Quapaw Tribe! Maybe they can give us the answers we are looking for! They can help us stop the

Council!"

Rose squeezed Geoffrey's hand and looked at Henry then at Chrissy, "We want you both to know that we are here and in this fight. We want to help solve this mystery and discover who killed James. We love him and want justice. Not only for him but for all those who have been hurt or killed due to the Council."

Geoffrey agreed, "We will help in whatever way we can. I will lay down my life to figure out what is going on and make whoever killed James and your father pay."

"Wait a minute," Chrissy interjected. "Although I am grateful for you both, I am not sure I can be here for this. My girls and I will be leaving first thing in the morning." She couldn't put her girls through this. It was too dangerous.

Henry felt his stomach drop to the floor. "Leaving?" He knew she was upset. He just wasn't sure why or what, but something caused her to panic. He could feel it.

"Yes. I am not even sure I believe this. No offense, Geoffrey and Rose, but this is a very farfetched story. I mean. Power is transferred by Stones to a Council of men that have been around for over a hundred years. I just don't know. And even if I did believe this, I still would want to leave. I can't stay here with my girls. I would never put them in danger."

Rose got up from her chair and leaned down on the floor by Chrissy, "Sweetheart, this isn't a made-up story. Some days I wish it were a story but believe me when I say it is not."

It had taken Henry a moment, but he realized that he agreed with Chrissy. "I think it would be best if you do leave. We would never want your girls or you caught up in this."

What are you hiding, Chrissy? Henry thought to himself. He could feel the sheer panic settling in with her. Something had set her off. But what? He thought back and realized she panicked as soon as Geoffrey said they needed someone with Quapaw blood. *Could that be it? Did Chrissy know someone with Quapaw blood?* Whoever it was, she seemed to want to protect them. That meant he would stay quiet.

"Before you leave, Chrissy, I need to tell you what I found out last night. I remembered the identity of one of the men in The Council, and I also found out another member's identity. I got a strange phone call from a friend we know as our local Postmaster, George Watkins." Geoffrey paused, trying to figure out the best way to tell her.

"George Watkins? What did he say that would have to do with me?" Chrissy could see the strain Geoffrey was under, "Just tell me. I can handle it."

"The Council has your mother."

CHAPTER 23

"The Council has my mother!?!" Chrissy shrieked. "Why would George Watkins tell you they have my mother? And where exactly can I find this Council?"

"George Watkins slipped away last night and called me. As I said, I didn't even realize he was a part of this. He has been our Postmaster for as long as I can remember and he became a good friend some twenty years ago. I would never have suspected he was involved with the Council members. He was in the process of telling me about your mother when something happened to him."

"What do you mean by something happened to him?"

"George had just told me that the Council had her when I heard a noise in the background. Then Ronald Burgess came on the line and asked me who he was speaking to. I hung up immediately. I can only imagine what he did to George."

Henry stood up and walked around the table, "Geoffrey, is that all he said, or is there more to it? And isn't Ronald Burgess the Mayor of Moon Lake?"

"Yes, Ronald Burgess is the Mayor. George said that The Council is up to something and that it involves you, Chrissy. He said he doesn't know exactly what is going on, but he knows something is. Then he said that Ronald Burgess kidnapped Jocelyn, and she has been living in some place he referred to as "the community" ever since. And that was the end of our conversation. Ronald had to have heard part of what was said."

"How can this be happening? I want to believe my mother is alive. Of course, I do, but how can I believe that she has been living in a community all this time without getting ahold of me? She has been missing since the year I graduated high school. Almost fifteen years now. She wouldn't let me suffer, thinking she was dead. I know she wouldn't."

"Chrissy, your poor mama may not have a choice. Remember that Ronald and the Council Members are powerful, and she may have had her memory taken away. Honey, why don't you take the afternoon and even tonight if you need it to think everything over? We know this is a lot to take in, and it's an almost unbelievable story, but please look at all the evidence before making a final decision." Rose had such a kind voice that it was hard to say no.

"Of course, Rose."

Henry sat back down across from Chrissy, "Will you please let me know before you go anywhere? It's not safe for you and the girls to be alone right now."

"Yes, but we will not be leaving The Lodge until tomorrow at the earliest," Chrissy said as she got up and walked over to the window, looking out at the early morning fog on the lake.

Henry joined her at the window, and they stood in silence for what seemed like forever before she spoke in a whisper, "Henry, can this all be for real?" Her voice sounded weak even to her own ears.

"I believe it can." He answered.

Chrissy turned towards Henry and was struck by the odd expression of guilt he had on his face. He looked almost like he wanted to tell her something. "Henry, do you have something you want to tell me?"

He met Chrissy's gaze and quickly lowered his eyes. "You know what, I do have something I want to tell you, but I don't think right now would be a good time. You have had enough to take in for one day, and what I must tell you doesn't have anything to do with Moon Lake. It's personal. But I promise you I will tell you if I see that I need to."

"Hey. Look at me." Chrissy felt a strong desire to comfort Henry.

He looked up, and she held her arms out for a hug. That exact moment is when he realized he was in love with her. He had never allowed himself to get this close to a woman, but at this point, there was no turning back. He loved Chrissy Bennett, and that was final.

He stepped into her embrace, and they stood like that for what seemed like an eternity before he spoke. "I should be the one comforting you. Not the other way around."

Chrissy stepped back and pulled her hair up into a ponytail, "I'm not the only one impacted here. I realize that. You lost a friend, now you've been pulled into this situation like an episode of The Twilight Zone. I would think it odd if you didn't need a bit of comforting."

They were interrupted by the doorbell ringing. A couple of minutes later, Rose appeared with a man in a police uniform walking with her.

The man walked towards Chrissy with an outstretched hand while Rose slipped out of the room. "Hello ma'am, I'm the local Sheriff, and I wanted to stop by and offer my condolences on the loss of your uncle. I am sorry I didn't make it to the memorial service. I was out of town on a case, and I'm just now returning."

Chrissy shook his hand, "Hello, I'm Chrissy Bennett." Lela and Jessica came running in, and Chrissy introduced them, "and these two streaks of lightning are my girls, Lela and Jessica."

"Hello, sir," Lela said with a smile. "Hi! Are you a Policeman?" Jessica asked.

"Hi, there, young ladies. I sure am a policeman, and it's my pleasure to meet you." He replied with a big smile.

Henry introduced himself, "Hello, Sheriff. I'm Henry Kesselberg."

"Kesselberg? Now that's an old school name. Where you from, Henry?" The sheriff inquired.

"My family originates from Germany."

Before the sheriff could continue his line of questions, Rose walked back into the room with Geoffrey in tow. Rose carried a platter of cookies, and Geoffrey had a tray with a teapot and several cups on it.

"We brought refreshments. Please help yourself, Sheriff."

"Thank you, ma'am. I believe I will." The sheriff grabbed a cookie and, in between bites, continued, "Listen, my wife would have my head if I didn't invite y'all over for dinner this coming up Friday night. We have a seven-year-old daughter and a nine-year-old son that would love to meet you, girls."

Chrissy was pleased that the local sheriff was so hospitable. "We would love to. I'm just not sure when we are leaving, but if we are still in town, we will accept your kind invitation."

"Please, mommy!" Both girls said almost in unison.

Chrissy noticed a look pass between Geoffrey and Rose. *I wonder what that's all about.*

"We will see." Chrissy gave the girls a pointed look that said, *don't ask again.*

"Well, I best get going." The sheriff said as he stood up, grabbing a couple more cookies. "How about I have my wife call The Lodge, say on Friday morning, to see if you folks are still in town? If so, I'll leave the dinner planning to you ladies."

"Sounds good, Sheriff. Thank you for stopping by."

"Yes, ma'am. By the way, I don't believe I formally introduced myself. I'm Sheriff Rollings, but you can call me Lucas."

CHAPTER 24

Henry watched Sheriff Lucas Rollings disappear inside the cave as he crouched behind the sheriff's cruiser. The sheriff had been careful to ensure that he wasn't followed, but he hadn't counted on someone following him on foot. And Henry was wearing black pants and a black t-shirt, so he blended in with the night.

Henry had sensed that Sheriff Rollings was up to no good the moment he walked in The Lodge. The sheriff had been friendly on the surface, but the way he truly felt emanated beneath his warm smile. Luckily for Henry, he was able to see right through his façade.

Chrissy had been impressed that he had stopped by, but Henry knew she was not too keen on visiting his home for dinner. Although it probably had less to do with the Sheriff and more to do with the situation they had found themselves in.

He pictured Chrissy's face and groaned. He knew he had to tell her the truth about his life, but he wasn't sure how. He dreaded it. She would make him leave. He just knew it.

Henry still couldn't believe the story Geoffrey told them was true, yet he didn't sense that Geoffrey was untruthful at any point in the conversation. *How could this have been happening without me knowing?* He thought for what seemed like the twentieth time.

Henry quickly moved to the front of the cruiser when he

saw bright headlights coming down the road. He could tell that the driver was in a big-time hurry, and he had to crouch lower when the black sedan slid to a stop on the other side of the sheriff's cruiser.

Henry heard the door slam, and he decided to look under the cruiser to see if he could tell who was in the sedan. Unfortunately, all he saw was a pair of brown dress shoes that appeared expensive and some brown slacks. Henry decided to get closer to see if he recognized the man, so he moved towards the sedan.

After making his way to the sedan, he peeked around the rear passenger side and saw a man disappear down the trail that led to the cave entrance. *Man! I have to get closer so I can see his face.* Henry knew how important it was to know who else was involved in The Council and decided it was worth the risk.

He listened for a couple more minutes before heading to the cave entrance. There was a ladder at the cave opening that appeared to lead to a pathway of sorts. He didn't think twice before climbing down the ladder.

Once he reached the bottom, he landed on the pathway and continued walking for a few minutes, being careful to make as little noise as possible. He could hear water running, so he knew there had to be an underground stream in the cave. After a short distance, he came upon a wooden bridge, and a stream was coming from another direction. As he was crossing the bridge, he saw an unexpectedly large waterfall.

He would have loved to spend some time taking in the view but couldn't risk getting caught, so he kept walking.

He slowed down when he heard voices echoing off the cave wall.

"What are our next steps?"

"It is imperative that we get the two girls before she can leave town with them."

"Agreed. I invited them over for dinner with me, my wife, and kids this Friday, and I believe we can set everything up at my house."

"Now Lucas, when did you run off and get a wife and kids? I had no idea you moved so fast."

"Don't you worry – I'll have a suitable wife and a couple of kids in place before Friday."

"Alight. What do you have in mind?"

"We can suggest that all the kids go outside and play, and we will ensure they go exploring and get lost in the woods. Oh, and we will for sure spend hours and hours searching. But, unfortunately, those woods are deep, and the dam is wide."

"Make it happen. Do whatever it takes to get the job done."

"You can count on me. I am the sheriff, after all."

Both men laughed and started walking towards the exit and Henry. When he heard their footsteps coming, he took off running and was out of the cave in mere seconds.

CHAPTER 25

C hrissy walked out of the kitchen with her steaming cup of Hot Cocoa and set it on the coffee table. From experience, she already knew she wouldn't be getting any sleep, so she may as well be productive.

She then walked over to the VCR and hit eject to remove the Scooby Doo movie her girls had fallen asleep watching.

She hesitated for a brief second before she slid the tape her mother had sent to her uncle in the slot. After she pressed play on the VCR, she curled up on the couch with a blanket. She looked over at her girls and felt her heart squeeze with love. They were both sound asleep on the recliner, all curled up and covered up with her mother's old throw.

Her mother's face appeared on the TV screen just as the doorbell rang. She looked at her watch and saw that it was almost 10:30 when Henry walked in with Geoffrey close behind him.

"Hi, Chrissy. I hate to show up so late, especially after all that's happened today, but what I have to tell you couldn't wait until morning."

Chrissy felt her stomach knot up, "What's wrong? Has something else happened?" She wasn't sure how much more she could take in one day.

"Yes. I have been following Sheriff Rollings ever since he

left The Lodge this morning."

"So that's why you left in such a hurry? I didn't even hear your Jeep leave the drive."

Chrissy noticed how Henry almost looked defeated. "How about we all sit down. Geoffrey, would you mind asking Rose to come in here? I would like to explain what I saw to all three of you."

Geoffrey headed down the hallway and was back with Rose in less than five minutes.

Chrissy had gone to the kitchen and walked back in a couple of minutes afterward with a tray full of cups of hot cocoa. "I figured I would get everyone some hot cocoa."

"Thank you, Chrissy."

"I followed Sherriff Rollings all day, and nothing major happened. That is until around nine tonight I hit the jackpot. He traveled around ten miles outside of town to a cave, and I watched as he disappeared into the cave. Before I could follow him inside, another car pulled up, and I hid until the other driver got out and entered the cave. I couldn't make out his face, so I waited a couple of minutes before going into the cave. I had to follow a trail, and after a few minutes, I heard voices, and I was able to hide and listen to part of their conversation."

"What did you hear?"

"They were discussing your girls."

"What do you mean, they were discussing my girls?" Chrissy shouted.

Lela set up, rubbing her eyes, "Mommy, what's wrong?"

"Oh, honey, I am so sorry. I shouldn't be yelling."

"It's ok, Mommy. Can I go to bed? I brushed my teeth already. Remember?"

"Yes, and I am glad you both brushed your teeth before turning on Scooby! Let's get you and your sissy to bed." She turned to Henry, "Don't say a word until I get back."

Henry watched them leave the room and was almost surprised when Rose sat down beside him and touched his arm. "We are thankful that you are here, Henry. Chrissy needs someone like you in her corner."

Chrissy walked back in and sat on the recliner the girls had vacated before looking at Henry. "I'm sorry I snapped at you. None of this is your fault, and you are helping so much. Please forgive me."

"Don't give it another thought."

Geoffrey took a sip of his hot cocoa as memories of a similar cave flooded his mind, "Henry, you said you heard them talking about Lela and Jessica when they were in the cave you followed them into. Did you happen to see a stream and waterfall in this cave?"

"Yes, there was a stream and waterfall both. Why do you ask?"

"Your description caused a memory to surface. The cave sounds like a place I spent a lot of time at in my past."

"I would assume it is the same. But what could this cave have to do with Chrissy's girls? The man that I couldn't identify was questioning Sheriff Rollings about their plan. He wanted to know where things stood, and the sheriff told him about inviting you over for dinner. Chrissy, they plan on making it seem like your girls get lost in the woods and are unable to be found. They want to kidnap your girls."

Chrissy gasped. "Why would they want to kidnap my girls? How would that benefit them?" As soon as the words left her mouth, she realized why. People had been coming up missing for years and years. People who had never been found. "I have to get my girls out of here."

Henry and Geoffrey exchanged a glance, "I will have to say that Geoffrey, Rose, and I all agree. Lela and Jessica need to be somewhere safe. Far from Moon Lake."

"I can take them to their grandparents in Florida. We will

leave first thing in the morning."

Henry wasn't about to let them make the drive alone. "I would like to come with you, Chrissy. You will need someone there to watch your back and to help make sure no one is following you."

"Yes, that is a great idea." Geoffrey agreed they would need protection.

"I agree that you coming with us would be best for the girls and everyone. The only concern I have is how I will explain your presence to my in-laws."

"How about we tell them the truth? That is that James's death was somehow tied to not only your grandmother's but also your father's. And that your mother is alive, and you need to find her? And that I am a friend of the family and am helping you get to the bottom of everything? How does that sound?"

"That would work. Honesty is the best policy, after all. Don't you agree, Henry?"

Henry felt like he had been punched in the gut. "I do." He walked over to the window and stared at the moon as it danced on the ripples in the lake.

Rose had heard the fear in Henry's voice, so she joined him at the window. "Isn't the moon just beautiful on the lake in an eerie sort of way?"

Henry jumped, and when Rose looked at him, she saw that he was petrified. "Henry, it will be ok."

"I feel like I could throw up, Rose. I don't know if I can have that conversation with Chrissy. She will hate me and make me leave. Or worse."

Rose patted his arm. "Now, Henry. I thought you had better sense than this. You have gotten to know Chrissy very well over the past couple of months. She will understand; you may just have to give her some time to accept it."

Rose smiled the most reassuring, supportive smile she

could muster at Henry, then walked over to Geoffrey and announced, "It is time for you and me to go to bed."

Geoffrey wasn't ready to go to bed. "I wanted to..." Rose cut him off quickly, "We can have a snack, honey, but then we are going straight to bed." She eyeballed him hard.

He seemed to get the message. "Bed does sound good, after all."

CHAPTER 26

Henry continued to stare at the moon and the lake, and Chrissy noticed he had a nervous edge in his voice when he spoke. "Are you up to us having a conversation tonight? I truly wanted to wait a while before filling you in, but I feel it's best to tell you the whole truth in light of our current circumstances. The sooner, the better."

Chrissy cringed. She knew he had been lying about something. "Sure thing. But before we start, I will need something stronger than hot cocoa. Would you like a cup of coffee?"

Henry breathed a sigh of relief. At least he had a few more minutes to figure out the best way to tell her his life story. A few more minutes to be in her life. So he figured he might as well make the best of them. "A cup of coffee sounds great, but only if I can help you in the kitchen."

Within ten minutes, they had their cups of coffee, had peeked in on the girls, and were back in front of the window overlooking the lake.

Chrissy's hands were sweating so hard she had to wipe them on her pants. She could tell that Henry was nervous, and it scared her. But, after everything she had already learned about the evil within Moon Lake, how bad could Henry's news be? Surely not worse than a group of men in Moon Lake with evil spirits living inside them who go around killing people.

Henry was feeding off Chrissy's emotions, and he knew

he better get himself under control, so he dove right in. "I need to tell you the truth about who I really am. What I am about to tell you will sound farfetched. Maybe even unreal. Please keep an open mind."

"Okayyyy. Now you are scaring me. Please tell me you are not on the FBI's Most Wanted List. I watch that show, you know." *Ugh, stop trying to be funny, Chrissy. Henry is serious and needs to talk. Don't make light of his situation.* "I'm sorry, Henry. I tend to joke when I get nervous. Please continue. I'm listening."

"I have only ever told one other person what I am about to share with you. This is not an easy tale to tell. Are you sure you want to hear this? I know this day has been full of stress and heartache. I don't want to add more to your stress. I've tried to prolong it, but I just don't know how to avoid having this conversation."

"I feel like I need to hear this. Tonight. I can take it." She knew this was a big deal.

Chrissy's eyes were fixed to Henry's face as he started telling his story. "My given name is Heinrich Martin Kesselberg. I was born to Lady Katarina Louise Fraunberg of the Province of Hanover, Germany, and her commoner husband, Heinrich Karl Kesselberg, in the year 1861."

Chrissy caught her breath. *I knew it.* "Are you telling me that you have been part of what is happening here in Moon Lake? That you have a conscience, so you have become a rogue Council Member? Or is it something else completely?"

"No! I had never even heard of The Council until Geoffrey told us about them." He paused, trying his best to work up the nerve to tell her the rest of the story. But, instead, he took a sip of the hot coffee – mainly to buy time. Then, knowing he couldn't avoid the truth, he continued.

"I am something else completely." Henry looked over at Chrissy, not quite meeting her eyes. "The only person I ever trusted enough with my life story was your Uncle James. I am now trusting you with the truth because I know you are an honorable woman and will not share what I say with another living soul."

Chrissy swallowed hard. "Of course not. I give you my word."

"My parents were on a picnic a few miles from home when a strange man came out of the woods and killed my father. He then attacked my mother and left her broken and bleeding in the middle of the woods."

Chrissy jumped to her feet and almost ran to Henry's side. She wanted to say something, anything, but when she opened her mouth to speak, she had no words. So instead, she held his hand.

Henry wanted to cry. Repeating the story of his father's death never got any easier. If only Chrissy knew how he needed the comfort of her touch. Her touch alone gave him the mental strength to continue with his story.

"My mother spent the next several days alone in the woods writhing in pain. She later told me she thought she was dead or on the brink of it, but death never came. Instead, she felt herself growing stronger as the days passed. She fed on small animals that were curious enough about her to get within her reach. Finally, when she had the strength to get up, she buried my father and made her way home."

"I am so sorry."

"I was away on holiday with my best friend when it happened. We were celebrating my twenty-first birthday. That's what I was doing when my parents were attacked. I should have been there!"

"There's no way you could have known. No way." *Wait. Why am I engaging in this conversation? This can't be true. Right? It is true. I knew it all along! Chrissy's emotions were still all over the place. Maybe Henry was right. Maybe she didn't need to hear this tonight. No. You are stronger than that. Now it's time to be even stronger than ever before.*

"I have come to realize that as time has gone by. But I still regret that I wasn't there to save my father's life." He paused for what seemed like ten minutes before he stood up and walked out the door.

Chrissy jumped up and followed him to the front door. "Hey! Where are you going?"

Henry looked at Chrissy, and her heart lurched at the raw pain she saw on his face. "Chrissy, I'm so sorry, but I have to go. My emotions are out of control – I promise I will be back."

Chrissy's mouth dropped open as she watched Henry disappear in a cloud of smoke.

CHAPTER 27

Chrissy stood at the front door, staring out at the dark night, when she heard footsteps coming up behind her. She turned, thinking Henry could have come back through the back, but instead, it was Rose standing there.

"I couldn't sleep, so I got up to make a cup of warm milk and honey. Want to join me?"

"I would love to."

"Ok, you get settled on the couch, and I will make our cups of milk and bring them in."

A few minutes later, they were sipping their warm honey milk wrapped up in blankets, watching an episode of "Mama's Family."

"I am here if you ever need to talk," Rose whispered.

"Thank you, Rose. I appreciate you so very much."

They sat in silence through the episode then Rose stood up. "I better get back to bed. Wake Geoffrey and me up if you need anything. I don't care what time of night it is."

"Will do. Good night."

"Try to get some rest. Good night, honey."

Chrissy headed to the kitchen to rinse out her cup and stopped dead in her tracks when she saw Henry standing in the foyer.

Her heart leaped in her throat. "You came back."

"I wasn't willing to let what happened cause me to run away from you. From us. I honestly believe I can help you if you let me after all I've told you."

"Will you please tell me the rest? I want to understand you." She tried her best to keep her voice calm.

Henry nodded his head and walked back to the window. Staring out at the peaceful waters of Moon Lake helped calm his nerves.

"My mother decided it would be best for us to move. Her late great-aunt had a small cottage in another part of Germany, and we moved in there shortly after she turned."

"Turned?"

"Yes. You will understand what I mean in a minute."

"Sorry – I get impatient to know everything. Please do continue."

"My grandparents had both passed away, so I kept our formal estate running and cared for. Most people thought she couldn't bear the grief of losing her husband, so people left her alone. My mother, well she continued to be the loving mother she had always been. Of course, she missed my father, but she had always been so strong and determined. She vowed not to let the evil that had been done to her ruin our lives, and she did a great job doing just that."

"How are you...well...what you are? A Vampire? When did this happen to you?" *So, this is true? I am buying all this, right? Yes. Yes, I am.*

"My mother turned me into an Immortal when I was 38 years old. She felt she didn't have a choice. I had been out riding, and a neighbor mistook me for an escaped convict and shot me. As if that wasn't bad enough, the shot spooked my horse Blaze, and she trampled me good. The man who had shot me didn't realize his mistake until after I fell off my horse. He put me on his wagon and carried me straight to my mother when he realized it was me he had shot."

Chrissy couldn't believe what she was hearing, but it was more that she couldn't believe Henry was telling her. On the other hand, she was glad he was telling her. "What happened next?"

"My mother saved my life. Even though it was not an easy decision for her to make. She had known the agony I would go through, but she couldn't bear losing her only son."

"What do you do for money? I mean, how do you make a living? What do you do every day? What do you eat? Do you kill people?" Chrissy felt bad firing off all those questions at once, but she had to know the answers.

"Let me answer your last questions first as I feel that one is the most important. No, I absolutely do not kill people. At least not humans. As far as eating, I eat anything I want to but must have blood to survive. Animal blood suffices, so I don't drink blood from humans. My favorite thing to eat is a rare steak. I was born into wealth, and I still have enough money to last as long as needed."

"Ok. You didn't tell me what you do every day."

"I travel. I fish. I like to hunt. I do a lot of different things. James and I met every year in Destin to go deep-sea fishing. I'm not sure how it will ever be the same without him."

"Who do you kill?"

Henry almost choked on his spit. "Say what?"

"You said you don't kill humans. I want to know who you *do* kill."

He should have known that little tidbit wouldn't get past her. "I kill rogue vampires. Before you ask, rogue vampires are the ones who don't have empathy for humans. They are the ones who hunt and kill humans for their blood. So my mother and I are what are called Sympathizers."

Chrissy swallowed hard. "Wait. Your mother. Where is your mother? Is she still alive? And what are Sympathizers?"

"As a matter of fact, my mother is very much still alive. Sympathizers value human life and devote a great deal of time and energy to keeping humans safe. To accomplish this, we have Vampire Sympathizer Covens in every state."

"Oh, wow. How do you have a what did you call them... Vampire Sympathizer Coven in every state? Who runs them? And Where is your mother now?"

"We have a Vampire Elder who is in charge of their Coven. My mother has been in Germany, but she is currently on her way to Arkansas as we speak."

"She's on her way to Arkansas?"

"Yes. I asked for her help. The situation here is dire, and we need all the help we can get."

Chrissy sat down and put her head in her hands. "My life has turned into a fairy tale. Is this really happening? A group of people is running around doing things to people that we aren't quite sure of exactly. All we know is that people are missing, and several of my family members have been killed. Oh, and my grandfather seems to have been alive long enough to have at least two families over fifty years apart. And now I find out the man who has brought me the most comfort over the past couple of months isn't a human. Have I already said this is crazy?"

"You have. Now can I ask you a question?"

Chrissy nodded, so Henry continued. "Why are you so calm after hearing my story? Why aren't you freaking out a little bit more?"

"Who says I'm not?"

"I can tell that your heartbeat has only really increased a little, and you aren't even nervous about being around me."

"Oh. I guess you're right. I suspected you were the Henry that Uncle James has known for many years when I saw you, but

I couldn't justify in my head how it could be possible. Then I noticed your strength, and you also admitted earlier tonight that you followed the sheriff on foot."

"Wow. You are more observant than I gave you credit for. And how did I admit that I followed the sheriff on foot?"

"You followed him without taking a vehicle. So I put two and two together."

Henry didn't know what to say, so he simply stared at Chrissy with his mouth hanging open.

Chrissy laughed. "Close your mouth, Henry. I am not as calm as I appear. Plus, I have accepted the fact that I'm in an episode of The Twilight Zone, and I realize I have to act as normal as possible to get through it."

Henry couldn't help but laugh with her. "This conversation went better than I had anticipated. So what do you say we continue it in the car after we drop Lela and Jessica off with their grandparents?"

"Sounds good. And Henry," Chrissy grabbed Henry's hand, "thank you for trusting me enough to share such a raw, sensitive piece of your life with me. And for calling your mother to help us with this situation. But please understand that my girls come first in my life, and I will not allow anyone to be in their lives who could hurt them. So I will ask that you say your goodbyes to them tomorrow because we will be going back home after this is over."

Henry knew he was going to be sick. For the first time in over a hundred years. "I understand. Good night, Chrissy."

CHAPTER 28

C hrissy waited until seven o'clock the following morning before calling her in-laws. It turned out that her mother-in-law, Anne, had left for Natchez, Mississippi, earlier that morning to spend a couple of days with her sister. She and her husband, Frank, had both been thrilled when Chrissy asked if they would keep the girls for a week or two. They made plans for Chrissy to meet Anne in Natchez later that night to drop the girls off.

Chrissy felt like a huge weight had been lifted after speaking with Anne. Keeping Lela and Jessica safe was her number one priority, and she breathed easier, knowing they would be far away from Moon Lake.

She couldn't believe it had only been a little over two months since she had gotten the phone call from her uncle's attorney. The dreadful phone call that had changed her life. She had been blissfully ignorant of any council, murder, sacrifice, and she had been perfectly happy. Well, maybe not perfectly. She'd been content. Content to raise her girls and be a single mother. Her girls. They made her world go around, and she loved them beyond words.

Meeting Henry had caused something to click in her heart. She wasn't quite sure how that happened. She wasn't looking for that. Quite the opposite. Now what? He is a VAMPIRE, for crying out loud. She couldn't have a relationship with him. Not even.

How would that even work? It couldn't. That's how. Not at all.

She thought the best route would be to ignore her budding feelings. Yes. That would be what she would do. Happy she had decided, she hummed a tune as she and the girls settled at a table in the dining room.

Then the subject which had occupied her thoughts walked in the room, and the decision she had made seemed ridiculous. She could no sooner ignore what she felt for Henry than she could ignore the nose on her face.

"Good morning, ladies."

How am I going to be alone with him in a car? What am I going to do? Act normal. Smile and be friendly. But not too friendly. Chrissy thought.

"Good morning! Good morning!" Lela sang.

Jessica jumped up and wrapped Henry's leg in a hug before running into the kitchen.

"Morning. I spoke with my mother-in-law, and we are meeting up in Mississippi at her sister's house. Are you sure you're up to going? Please don't feel like you have to."

"If I didn't know better, I'd think you were trying to talk me out of going with you. Is there something you want to tell me?" Henry knew she was nervous due to finding him attractive, and he almost felt bad giving her a hard time. Almost.

"Ummm. No. I mean, not at all. Can you be ready by ten o'clock?" She stammered.

"You bet I can."

Rose came in from the kitchen carrying a couple of bags and handed them to Chrissy. "I made y'all some snacks for the road. There are sandwiches, chips, and some sliced vegetables in the brown bag and some cookies in this small bag."

Chrissy took the bags and smiled up at Rose. "Rose, I honestly don't know what we would do without you."

"Oh, fiddlesticks. I think you would be just fine."

"I disagree," Geoffrey stated as he walked in from outside and straight over to hug Rose. "And I sure hope I never have to find out!"

"I second that motion!" Chrissy was startled when she realized that she meant it. She wasn't quite sure how Rose and Geoffrey had come to mean so much to her in such a short time. Then she smiled to herself when the words "kindness, selflessness, welcoming, loving" all came to mind. That's how. They cared about people and weren't afraid to show it.

Chrissy found herself wondering if it wasn't time for her to take a page out of their book.

Chrissy glanced down at her watch and saw that she still had around an hour before they were leaving for Mississippi. The girls had their Barbie dolls happily chatting about spending time with their grandparents in Florida, so she decided to go outside and explore a little. The girls tagged along and settled in with their Barbies on a bench by the tool shed.

Chrissy walked inside the tool shed and was blown away when she saw her daddy's car still there underneath the tarp he had always insisted on using. She sat down in a plastic chair and allowed her mind to drift back to another time that she had blocked out for many, many years.

She was outside playing in a sprinkler beside the tool shed at The Lodge when she was seven years old. She remembered laughing and being so happy to have the cool water hit her in the face.

She heard her daddy from inside the tool shed. His voice was raised. She had found that odd because he was always so calm, and he hardly ever raised his voice. She had walked over to the tool shed and saw her daddy standing in front of his car with her Uncle James.

"So, you have known all along that Chrissy isn't yours?" Her Uncle James had asked her daddy.

"Yes, James. I have known all along. Jocelyn was pregnant when we reconnected." Then her Uncle James had interrupted him. "I can't believe this. Why didn't you tell me before now?"

"Jocelyn and I decided to keep the matter of Chrissy's paternity to ourselves. She had lost her husband and had nowhere to turn when she moved back to Moon Lake."

"But I'm your brother, Allen. You could have told me. Of all people, you could have trusted me."

"Jocelyn was worried people would look at Chrissy differently if they knew she was half Quapaw Indian. You know I had loved Jocelyn when we were in high school. Do you remember how devastated I was when her family moved to Oklahoma when we were seniors?"

"Yes. I do remember."

"Please tell me you don't look at Chrissy any differently. She is my daughter and your niece, and she always will be. I couldn't love her more than I already do, no matter what. I need you to promise me. Promise me nothing has changed, and you will take care of her if anything ever happens to me."

"I could never and would never look at her differently. I love her, Allen, and that hasn't changed. You have my word. If anything ever happens, I will be here for her."

She watched her daddy hug her Uncle, and she walked back to the sprinkler. It wasn't as fun as it had been before she overheard them talking, but she didn't know what else to do.

"Mommy! Are you sleeping?" She opened her eyes to see Jessica a half inch from her face.

"No, honey. Mommy was just thinking." She reached down and pulled Jessica in her lap, and kissed her cheek. Lela saw it and came running. "Dog pile!!!" she screamed as she jumped on top of Jessica.

They were still laughing when Henry walked into the tool shed. "Henry! We are having a dog pile!" Jessica screamed.

"I see that! I was wondering what all the commotion was

coming from the shed!" He couldn't help but laugh with them. He looked over at Chrissy and ultimately lost his senses. Her face was flushed, and she looked so happy with her girls on her lap.

Ok. I love her. I have to face it and decide how to handle it.

Then Jessica ran over and grabbed his hand, "Do you want to dog pile with us?"

Ok. I love them all. It's not just about Chrissy. These two little girls have stolen my heart as well.

"Henryyyyy! Are you listening to me? You didn't answer me. Do you want to dog pile with us?"

Henry leaned down and ruffled Jessica's hair. "I better not dog pile right now. I don't think that rickety chair could hold all of us! I came by to grab your bags and get the Tahoe loaded."

"We're going to grandma's!" Jessica sang as she ran into the lodge, with Lela on her heels singing along.

"You about ready to head out? Are you sure you are comfortable with me going with you?"

"Why wouldn't I be?" She smiled. "It's not like you told me anything far-fetched last night."

"You know. What I told you last night has to be hard on you. I don't want you doing anything that will cause you to be uncomfortable. But then, on the other hand, I want to be there in case anything happens and you need me."

"I don't feel the least bit uncomfortable. Uncle James told me that I could trust you with my life in the letter he left me, and I believe him. He would never, ever put the girls or me in danger."

"Did he? I believe you left that part out when you read the letter to me! I'll get the Tahoe loaded, then and meet you out front." Henry wasn't sure how he got so lucky for her to trust him still. Even after she found out his history, even knowing he wasn't who he seemed to be—just another reason for him to love her even more.

"Give me a few minutes to put our evidence back in the

secret spot, and the girls and I will be right out." Chrissy wanted to ensure everything was safe and well-hidden while they were gone.

CHAPTER 29

Sharon Malone watched as Sheriff Lucas Rollings quietly closed the door to her room at the Homeless Shelter. She felt a touch of excitement, knowing that she was close to finding out and putting a stop to what was going on in Moon Lake.

It had been almost twenty years since her little sister had been kidnapped after running away with a boy she met from Moon Lake. Twenty years that Sharon had lived with that loss. Twenty years of living with the guilt. Why her sister and not her? It should have been her. They had liked the same boy, and he had asked Sharon to run away with him. She had said no. Brenda had said yes.

Sharon and Brenda had been orphans, raised in the same foster home. They had met when Sharon was six and Brenda was five. Sharon had been the stronger one and had taken Brenda under her wing. Their foster mom had been abusive, and Sharon and Brenda had planned on running away someday.

When Sharon was seventeen and Brenda was sixteen, a boy named Jeremy had been placed in the same foster home. He was from Moon Lake, and he always said he couldn't wait to go back home to find his family. He was almost eighteen and, man, was he a looker! Both Sharon and Brenda had a crush on him, and they had started competing for his attention.

Robert paid more attention to Sharon at first, but when he asked her to run away with him, she couldn't bear the thought of leaving Brenda behind. She should have known he would ask Brenda. How could she have been so blind? It was her fault that Brenda left!

Sharon had ended up running away within a few months of her sister leaving. She went to Moon Lake and searched all over for her sister and Robert.

She stayed at the Homeless Shelter and pretended to be eighteen. That is until she had a horrible experience that shook her to her core.

A man had tried to kidnap her from the cafeteria one night. She had gone in there looking for something to snack on, and he had grabbed her. He covered her mouth and started saying weird stuff in another language, and she had felt her body going all weird.

The only thing that stopped him was a group of people walking in the cafeteria. He had shoved her down and ran out through the kitchen.

Sharon had gone straight to Miss Beth, who was in charge, and they had called the police. Only the police didn't believe her. They acted like she was a liar.

If not for Miss Beth, Sharon thinks she would have been killed that night. Miss Beth had borrowed a car from her neighbor and had driven her to Little Rock, Arkansas, to another shelter. She had stayed there for a few months and fell in with the wrong crowd.

After a few years of self-destructing, Sharon finally had gotten her stuff together. Of course, she had consequences that she dealt with, but at least one good thing had come out of her bad choices. She had met the love of her life. He had pulled her out of the self-destructive state she was in and helped her see the road she was on led to nothing but heartache and misery.

She had eventually learned to deal with the consequences of her past and even embrace them. Not that she had much choice.

Getting a job as an Investigative Reporter for the Little Rock Times was pure luck. It had given her access to research she wouldn't have had otherwise. She already knew something was going on in Moon Lake. But after spending time researching, she had no doubt left in her. Moon Lake, Arkansas had some major secrets. Secrets that could tear the town of Moon Lake and even the state of Arkansas apart if they were to come to light.

A man from Moon Lake had shown up at their office a few months earlier asking questions about news stories featuring missing people from Moon Lake over a hundred-year period. Her editor had been looking to assign her co-worker Brandon Penn to the story of Moon Lake missing people because he thought it may be too dangerous for a woman. As if.

Getting her editor to allow her to come to Moon Lake to cover the story instead of Brandon took some maneuvering. That was the easy part. But, lying and deceiving her husband was a different story. He would have never allowed her to come to Moon Lake undercover if she had told him the truth. Especially knowing she would be staying at a homeless shelter doing everything she could to get kidnapped.

The Sheriff sneaking in her room told her that her plan worked. She was going to be the next "victim," and she honestly could not wait.

CHAPTER 30

The six-hour drive to Natchez had actually been kinda fun. Henry and the girls had sung songs for a good part of the drive, and then they had all played I spy before the girls had both passed out.

The girls were so happy to see their grandma, and when she asked if Chrissy would consider allowing the girls to spend two weeks instead of just one week so they could go to Disneyworld, they were beyond thrilled. Of course, Chrissy had also been beyond thrilled, knowing they would be safe and far away from Moon Lake, Arkansas.

Henry had been polite and made a good impression, but Chrissy saw her mother-in-law looking at her and then him with a sly smile. It made her wonder if her mother-in-law would be on board with her dating someone else. Not that it mattered, she told herself. She had no intention of dating Henry or anyone else right now.

They stopped at a Burger King drive-through before starting on the drive back to Moon Lake, and Chrissy decided to share her memory with Henry. "I have something I need to tell you about my past."

Henry looked at her as he pulled out of the Burger King drive. "Alright."

Chrissy took a deep breath then recounted everything she could remember of the day her daddy and uncle were in the garage talking about her not being his biological daughter.

"Now your reaction when Geoffrey mentioned the Quapaw Indians makes sense."

"You noticed that, huh?"

"I did notice. But there's not a lot about you that I don't notice." *So why did I go and say that to her?*

Chrissy felt a blush coming on. "Henry...."

"I'm sorry. I shouldn't have gone there. I just can't seem to help myself when it comes to you." He knew he would have to keep his feelings to himself or scare her off.

"You didn't let me finish. Henry, I have certain feelings regarding you, too, but I have not worked them all out in my head. I would like to, though."

"Chrissy, I know we are different. Maybe even too different, but I am having a hard time putting a stop to my feelings. I have tried." He looked over at her to see if he could gauge how she felt about what he just said. He didn't feel any fear, and that was a plus.

"I can't make any promises. But I will say that I would at least like to spend time with you after all this is over so we can see where it goes."

YES! "I can agree to that." He tried not to show too much excitement, but it was hard. He felt like a teenager again, and it had been a VERY long time since he had felt like a teenager.

They had driven around an hour from Mississippi when Chrissy made a decision. "Henry, will you stop at the next gas station so I can buy a map? I think we need to go to Oklahoma so we can find the Quapaw Tribe. At this point, they may be the only ones who can help us. What if there is someone there that knows how to use the Stones to put the evil spirits back?" She cringed. "By the way, I can't believe I just said that out loud."

"You must be reading my mind. I was just thinking the same thing. Not about the map since I already know the way to Oklahoma, but about going to find the Quapaw tribe. It's around a ten-hour drive, so you may as well get some rest. If I drive through the night, we will be there early in the morning. Or we can drive halfway there and stop at a hotel." He clicked the blinker to turn into a gas station. "We also need to stop at a phone booth so we can call Geoffrey and Rose and fill them in."

Chrissy smiled at Henry and nodded her head, unable to find her voice. After making the call, she spent the next hour looking out the window with a ball of anxiety in her stomach. She wasn't sure if what she was feeling was relief at having decided to go to Oklahoma or fear. Not precisely fear of The Council and what they were facing, but fear of seeing the Quapaw. Seeing her kinfolk and not knowing if she should say something or not.

They decided to stop at a Holiday Inn so Chrissy could get some real rest after they had driven close to six hours. Henry opted to stay with the Tahoe so he could keep guard throughout the night.

CHAPTER 31

Panic surged through Lucas Rollings as he looked up at Ronald Burgess's angry face from the conference room floor. He couldn't remember a time in his life when he had ever felt a fear like he did at this very moment. Not ever.

He struggled against Ronald's hands, desperate for a breath. The look on Ronald's face told him that he was going to die. He was sure of it.

The shock mixed with relief he felt when Ronald removed his hands from his throat and walked away was almost surreal.

"Lucas, I am extremely disappointed in you. You have shown yourself to be unreliable. First, you fail to tell me that my great-granddaughter has the man I've had my eye on these past few years, Henry Kesselberg, with her, then you let them leave town with those girls. How? I thought you understood the importance of having them in The Community. Your incompetence has cost me more than you realize." Ronald was furious. He had wanted to take those girls to Jocelyn and let her keep them until the time for sacrifice. For some reason, she wanted to adopt a kid, so why not let her get it out of her system? He was confident she would be willing to forgive him for their sacrifice when the time came. Especially after she got a taste of immortality!

"I'm sorry, Ronald. I didn't know it was important to mention Henry Kesselberg, and I told you I got pulled away for police business. How could the sheriff very well decline to help with an automobile accident when the dispatcher knew I was within a mile of the scene? It wouldn't have looked good, and you know it." Lucas tried to reason with Ronald.

"I don't want to hear any more of your pitiful excuses. Your new assignment is to kill Henry Kesselberg. There's more to him than meets the eye, and I don't want him messing up our plans. After he is dead, you are to bring Chrissy and those girls to me then. Do you understand what I am asking you to do?"

"Yes. Ronald, I do. I won't mess up again. I give you my word."

"You had better not, or you will find yourself in an awful situation."

Katarina Kesselberg quietly closed the door to Mayor's office and started down the long hallway when an older blonde woman stopped her.

"May I help you with something?" the blonde woman asked her.

Katarina looked at her name tag and saw that she was the mayor's secretary. "Oh, hi. I am new in town and wanted to stop by and meet the Mayor." Katarina smiled the warmest, most friendly smile she could muster at the woman.

"How nice of you to stop by. I'm Mrs. Sarah Washington, the Mayor's secretary. Our Mayor, Mr. Burgess, is in a meeting with our Sheriff." The receptionist said, smiling back at Katarina. She looked down at a booklet on her desk and said, "He is free this afternoon at 3:30, and you are more than welcome to stop back by."

"Thank you so much, Mrs. Washington. I may do just that." Katarina turned on her heel and walked out the front door before the secretary could ask for her name.

Katarina now understood why Henry had called and

asked her to come to the Lodge. After hearing the exchange between the Mayor and Sheriff, she knew they had a battle ahead of them. She was very thankful she had driven straight to Moon Lake from the airport in Little Rock when she arrived.

Otherwise, she would have missed the Sheriff on his stakeout of the Lodge.

She had grown suspicious when she noticed a man in a cop car sitting out of sight from the Lodge. He had a pair of binoculars up to his face looking straight at the Lodge, and she then knew for a fact that he was watching the people at the Lodge.

Following him when he pulled out a few minutes later was like second nature to Katarina as she had grown into a suspicious person over the years. If she hadn't followed him, she would not know the extent that Henry was in danger. Or the woman Chrissy and her girls. Even though she had never met them, she could tell Henry cared for them, and Katarina knew she would do what it took to keep them safe.

CHAPTER 32

Henry looked at his watch as he pulled into an Exxon station right out of Ottawa County in Oklahoma. He smiled as he heard Chrissy's even breathing never miss a beat. She had spent the past hour napping with her head laying on a rolled-up sweater against the window.

It was close to eleven o'clock in the morning, so he figured he could get gas and then wake Chrissy so they could both get freshened up after being on the road the past few hours.

He looked over at her sleeping so peacefully and felt his heart clench with love. He was glad that he finally accepted that he loved her. He simply couldn't deny it. He loved her. He was still looking at her when she cracked open one eye and yawned. "Where are we?"

"Around an hour from the town of Quapaw. I figured we could freshen up and get something to eat here before we drive on into Quapaw."

"Yes. Food sounds wonderful. And I will call and check on the girls."

Her stomach was doing flip-flops. Not because she was hungry, of course, it couldn't be that simple. Nope. It had to be complicated. Way more complicated. Because it had to do with Henry and the way he was looking at her when she woke up. It made her feel safe. Protected. Loved. *Loved! Henry doesn't love me. How could he? He has this exciting life while I am a regular, bor-*

ing lady who has no excitement. At least not like he has. Her mind was running away with her when Henry's face appeared in her window.

"Come on, sleepyhead. Let's go grab something to eat and get cleaned up." He walked around to the driver's side and got in so he could park.

An hour later, they pulled onto Highway 71 headed for Quapaw, Oklahoma, and hopefully, answers.

"Henry! Do you see the Buffalo? There are several in that field over there!"

"Yes, they are a sight to behold, that's for sure."

"That was cool. Ok, where to first? We should find their City Hall or something, shouldn't we?"

Henry looked down the road, "There's a store up the road. Let's stop there and ask."

A few minutes later, they pulled into the drive outside a square and plank building painted red with blue shutters. They walked in and were welcomed by a woman that looked to be in her mid to late fifties. "Hello and welcome to my shop. I am Anne Buffalo, and I am happy you have decided to stop by. What can I help you find?"

Henry inquired about who they could speak to that would know history from when the Quapaw Tribe lived in Arkansas, and Anne Byrd directed them to the Main Street Café. She said many elderly gentlemen met in there to drink coffee and swap stories in the mornings and, on occasion, hang out until after lunch.

Meanwhile, a wall of velvet bags caught Chrissy's attention, and when she got up closer, she realized why. They had the exact same designs as the velvet bag the Stones were in. Chrissy saw the only difference was the moonstone on the front of the bags were smaller; the feathers looked different, and some of them had painted pictures in place of the moonstone.

"Excuse me, ma'am. Who made these beautiful bags?"

She smiled proudly, "Those are all handmade by my Grandfather."

"Wow, they are extremely well done."

"He is very gifted, no?"

"Yes, he sure is. I will take one. Do you mind telling me his name? And do you know if your Grandfather would happen to be at the Café today? I would love to speak to him about these."

The woman looked puzzled as if she wondered why in the world anyone would want to ask her Grandfather about his velvet pouches. Still, she told Chrissy his name was Joseph Byrd and that he was generally at the Café until at least ten o'clock every morning and that he returned most days for lunch.

Chrissy ended up purchasing the bag and a pair of beautiful moccasins before they headed out for the Main Street Café.

Once they got in the car, Chrissy pointed out how the bags in the shop looked exactly like the ones that held the stones, and Henry agreed it was no coincidence.

CHAPTER 33

Chrissy followed Henry into the Main Street Café, where they were greeted by a friendly man who asked them to seat themselves. They went ahead and sat at a booth. Both were looking around to see if the people they were looking for were even at the Café.

The waitress came by and asked them what she could get them, and Chrissy and Henry both ordered a cup of coffee. Before she left to get their coffee, Henry asked her if any elderly gentlemen were gathered in the Café that day for lunch. He thanked her when she pointed towards another room off the main area.

While waiting on their coffee, Chrissy felt they needed a plan. "What are we going to say when we go in there? Do you have a plan?"

"Yes. I am going to ask to speak to Joseph Byrd about his handmade velvet pouches. Then we will see what he says and go from there."

"So, you don't have a plan, huh?"

Henry grabbed her hand, "Come on; we will figure it out together."

There was a large round table in the middle of the other room with three older men sitting at it, and Henry walked straight up to them.

"Hello, gentlemen. I'm Henry Kesselberg, and this is

Chrissy Bennett. We have driven several hours to speak with you. May we join you?"

The largest of the three stood up and pulled out a chair for Chrissy. "We are not in the business of saying no to a pretty woman, now, are we?"

The other two spoke up and welcomed Henry and Chrissy to join them. They exchanged names and learned the polite man who pulled out the chair for Chrissy was Lloyd Buffalo, John Whitebear was sitting on the opposite side to him, and both Henry and Chrissy were happy to hear the last one was Joseph Byrd.

"So, what is so important that had you driving so many hours that you think we can help you with?" John Whitebear asked.

Henry glanced over at Chrissy before answering. They might as well lay it all out there. "There is something strange going on in Moon Lake, Arkansas, and we have come to ask for your help in figuring the situation out."

All three men at the table exchanged a glance before Joseph Byrd spoke up. "Moon Lake, Arkansas, you say? What exactly do you think is going on there?"

"I don't know how to say it without sounding crazy. So I will just say it. We don't know exactly what is going on. All we know is that people have been disappearing almost every month for the past fifty-plus years, and they are never found. One man named Bradley Whitmore has been linked to these disappearances, but he is now also dead. Chrissy's grandmother was killed long before Chrissy was born. Her father, Allen Kensington, was found dead a few years later. Her mother, Jocelyn Kensington, went missing the year Chrissy graduated from high school, and now her uncle James Kensington has recently been killed. They left evidence behind that points to an evil group of men at the center of the situation."

Joseph Byrd looked at Henry before settling his eyes on

Chrissy. "Did I hear you right?" He leaned closer to Chrissy. "Jocelyn Kensington is your mother?"

"Yes, sir. Why do you ask? Did you know her?" Chrissy had an uneasy feeling in the pit of her stomach.

Joseph looked at her with tears in his eyes. "What year were you born?"

The uneasy feeling in the pit of her stomach grew by leaps and bounds. "I was born in May of 1964. What does that have to do with anything?" She asked the question even though she had a sinking feeling it had everything to do with *everything.*

Joseph Byrd looked at Chrissy as if he were trying to see her soul. It seemed like an hour had passed when he finally spoke. "Jocelyn Kensington was once known as Jocelyn Byrd. You see, she was married to my son, Louis until he passed from this life in 1963."

Chrissy's head was spinning. Could this man be her Grandfather? She felt an arm around her shoulders and was thankful that Henry had scooted his chair over by hers. "Are you positive this is the same Jocelyn?" Of course, she already knew it was, but she had to ask.

"Yes, my child. My son left your mother a young, pregnant widow. When she reconnected with her old high school boyfriend from back in Arkansas and became engaged, I gave my blessing. Dear child, her old high school boyfriend's name was Allen Kensington."

Chrissy felt Henry's arm tighten around her, and she drew strength from his embrace. "So, you are my Grandfather? And you knew about me? Why is this the first time I am meeting you?"

"Allen Kensington promised me he would take care of Jocelyn and her child. He promised that he would raise you as his own, and he asked me to allow them to raise you in peace. He did not want interference from my family or me. I knew that was the best chance Jocelyn had at making a life for you without big struggles. So, I agreed to stay out of your life. Please, forgive me." The tears from his eyes had spilled down his cheeks, and Chrissy's heart went out to him.

Chrissy felt panic start to overtake her. Even though her heart ached for the man in front of her, she wasn't ready for this. She needed to get away from him. From this reality that had been shoved down her throat ever since her uncle had died. Away from the man with tears rolling down his cheeks, looking at her like he loved her. He didn't even know her. She pushed away from the table and ran out the front door.

By the time she reached the vehicle and realized Henry had the keys, she could no longer keep everything bottled in. Tears welled from deep inside her, coursing down her cheeks as she fell to the ground beside her Tahoe.

She had barely hit the ground when strong arms picked her up and held her close. She knew it was Henry, and she clung to his neck as if he was a lifejacket and she was deep under the water drowning.

CHAPTER 34

Henry held Chrissy until her tears dried up and she was prepared to face her new reality. Then, when she pulled away from him and looked up into his eyes, he caught his breath. He could feel her love for him, and he was blown away.

He could not have stopped himself from leaning down and pressing his lips to hers no more than he could stop himself from loving her. He only wanted to offer comfort, and he hoped she took it as that. When he stepped back and saw the look on her face, he knew she had needed that comfort.

Chrissy was shocked at how she could go from a deep need to cry her eyes out to a deep need to confess her love for Henry within a matter of seconds. She was ready to admit she loved him but knew that she was not even close to prepared to do something about it, so she kept her mouth shut tight.

"Did my bad behavior scare them off? They must think I am a basket case."

Henry leaned down and pecked her on the lips one more time before he answered her. "Not at all. They were so happy to see you, and they understood your reaction. It's not every day you meet the Grandfather you didn't know you had for the first time. Without any warning."

"Shall we go back in?"

"Your Grandfather, or shall I call him Mr. Byrd, asked us to meet him at his place. He thought it would be best if we have privacy for this conversation. And I agreed."

A few minutes later, they found themselves knocking on the front door of a small, white house.

Joseph Byrd answered the door and invited them in.

"Please make yourselves comfortable. Can I get you some tea or water?" He asked them both, but his eyes were fixed on Chrissy's face.

Chrissy nodded as she sat on one end of the sofa. "Yes, we would both love some tea. Thank you."

He jumped up with a big smile on his face and headed to the kitchen. He looked like getting them some tea made him happy, so she was glad she said yes.

He returned with their tea and settled into a worn recliner across from the sofa.

"Dear Chrissy, I would love to get to know you better, but I fear now is not the time. First, we must discuss what you said brought you to see us. You said there is something strange going on in Moon Lake. Please, tell me more."

Together, Henry and Chrissy relayed everything they knew to Joseph.

Once they were finished, Joseph put his head in his hands. "The story of the Great Shaman Protector keeping evil spirits away has been told for many generations. Yet, all these years, I thought it was just a made-up story. I will tell you what I have grown up hearing, and we can go from there." He got up from the recliner and stood in front of the window, looking out as if he had transported back to another time.

"The story is that long, long ago, there were men who came to us from faraway lands by boat. They were explorers. Some of the Tribes welcomed these men, but not all of them. There was fighting and much death before these men left on their boats. The story has it that some evil spirits left with them. They were gone around two years before they returned. When they returned, they brought back and released the evil spirits on all the Indian Tribes in Arkansas. There was much more killing and much death before their Shaman Kaní ttą́ka put magic in simple stones that could contain the evil spirits."

Joseph walked back to his recliner and sat down before continuing. "The story says the Shaman had to fight the evil spirits and force them into the Stones."

He took a sip of tea and continued. "The Shaman realized he had made a mistake in trying to defeat the evil spirits alone. That is when he asked for help from other tribes and peoples."

Chrissy couldn't stand it. She had to ask. "What other people?"

"My dear child, he needed help from other people not of his descent. He had volunteers from different tribes, and he even had volunteers from the group of people who had traveled to take the land. Once he had gathered a group of volunteer warriors, they went back into battle and defeated the evil spirits.

The evil spirits were cast into the Stones, and the Shaman ending up locking himself in the cave with the Stones as the Great Eternal Guardian. The story says that the evil spirits should not have been able to escape. Do you know for sure they are no longer in the Stones?"

"Yes, we are certain. There is no other explanation." Chrissy felt confident the evil spirits had been causing all the disappearances and death over the years in Moon Lake.

"Ok. Then we need to go back to Moon Lake and see what we are up against. But, first, I will need to find the cave where the Shaman went to live out his eternity. There are more than likely some clues there that can help us defeat these evil spirits."

"Wait. We? You are going to Moon Lake with us?"

"I am. There's no way I would let my granddaughter fight these evil spirits without me." He paused and looked over at

Henry. "Even if she does have someone near invincible like you, Henry by her side."

Henry was speechless.

CHAPTER 35

Rose had just rinsed her Purple Hull Peas and poured them in a tall pot to boil when the phone rang. She hurriedly wiped her hands off on a towel and picked up the phone, "Hello. The Lodge, Rose speaking."

She was thrilled to hear Chrissy on the other line. "Hi, Rose. How are things there?"

"Oh, Chrissy, we are doing simply great. There hasn't been anything out of the normal happen, so that's a blessing."

"Yes, ma'am, that is for sure. But, listen, Henry is wondering if he has had anyone come by to see him. He's expecting some family to come in."

"We haven't had any visitors as of yet." As she answered, she heard a car coming down the drive. "Well, hold on a minute. We have someone pulling up right now."

Rose went to the window and saw Geoffrey speaking to a woman with long, blonde hair, so she hurried back to the phone. "Chrissy, there's a woman out front with long blonde hair speaking to Geoffrey."

"That's good. That must be Katarina. Will you let her know we are leaving Oklahoma and will be there later this afternoon?"

"I sure will. I can run outside and get her if you want to speak to her."

"Please. I know Henry is anxious to talk to her."

Rose looked out the window and saw that Geoffrey and Katarina were still outside, so she walked to the front door. "Christmas will get here before you bring our guest inside, Geoffrey! Henry and Chrissy are on the phone waiting to talk to her!"

Katarina walked up to the door and looked at it expectantly. Rose opened it all the way and stepped aside. "Come on in and grab the phone. We can introduce ourselves afterward. Long-distance rates are not cheap!"

Rose handed Katarina the phone as soon as they got in the kitchen.

Geoffrey put his arms around her, "Mmmmm, whatever you are cooking smells so good! I can't wait for supper!" He kissed her on the cheek and walked towards the Dining Room.

Rose only halfway heard him and didn't respond. She was too busy listening to what the blonde woman was saying. All she heard was, "This man wants you out of the way, Henry. Please be careful driving in. I'll do some digging and see if I can find out more."

She couldn't stand it. She had to know who wanted Henry out of the way. It had to be someone on that stupid council again. Would they ever get away from them?

Rose was lost in thought and didn't hear the blonde woman hang the phone up. It took Geoffrey clearing his throat to get her attention.

"Penny for your thoughts." The blonde woman said with a smile.

Rose instantly liked her. "I often get lost in my thoughts. By the way, I am Rose Hamilton. I see you've met my husband, Geoffrey. Welcome to the Lodge." Rose took Katarina's hand and squeezed it.

"Hello, Mrs. Rose. I'm Katarina Kesselberg. It's nice to meet you finally. Henry has told me nothing but good things about you and your kind husband over the years." Katarina gently squeezed Rose's hand.

"Bless his heart. It is such a blessing to know him." Rose said as she grabbed a bag of Corn Meal out of the pantry. "Kesselberg. You must be Henry's sister."

Katarina shook her head. "Not exactly, but we are close kin."

Rose wanted to know more about their connection but decided to find out who was planning to harm Henry was a more pressing matter. "May I call you Katarina?"

Katarina nodded, so Rose continued. "You know Henry means the world to both me and Geoffrey. I couldn't help but overhear you on the phone. If someone wants to harm Henry, please let us know so we can help."

Geoffrey heard Rose from the Dining Room. "What's going on with Henry?" He asked as he walked back into the kitchen.

Katarina was surprised at the genuine care she felt from these two. She could tell that they were both honest, and it was refreshing. Not to mention Henry had already told her they were aware of the situation. So, she went ahead and filled them in on what had transpired, starting with seeing the sheriff watching The Lodge with a pair of binoculars and ending with her chat with the secretary.

Geoffrey opened his mouth to speak, but Rose beat him to it. "Those slimy weasels!"

Katarina then let them know Chrissy and Henry were bringing a Quapaw Indian descendant by the name of Joseph Byrd with them.

"That's good." Geoffrey had his fists balled up at his sides. "We need to do whatever it takes to put a stop to Ronald Burgess. Hopefully, the gentleman, Joseph Byrd, will be able to help us. It's a good start, anyway."

"Henry told me some of what is going on here, but I would

love to hear more from you two."

"I'll get us some refreshments, and we can go to the Main Room, so we are more comfortable." Rose handed Geoffrey a pitcher of tea, and she grabbed some glasses and a platter of chocolate chip cookies, and they made their way to the Main Room.

Geoffrey and Rose told Katarina everything they knew about The Council, and they all agreed it was past time to put an end to The Council and all its members.

They had stayed in the Great Room discussing strategies for around an hour before they decided to finish the conversation after Henry, Chrissy, and Joseph Byrd arrived.

Geoffrey and Rose had offered Katarina a room at The Lodge since Henry's cabin only had one bedroom, and she had accepted.

She was sitting on the bed looking out at the lake, thinking how the view was beautiful when she heard something that sounded out of place. She realized it was coming from down the road, so she got up to investigate.

A few minutes later, she found the source of the sound. The sheriff was under Henry's Jeep doing something that she couldn't see. She looked in his vehicle as she passed and saw wires, wire cutters, and plastic pieces in the front seat. From all appearances, this man was planting a homemade car bomb under Henry's Jeep.

Anger coursed through her body like a wildfire, and she grabbed the sheriff by his boots, quickly dragging him out from underneath the Jeep.

"What the..." Lucas Rollings looked up and saw something he never dreamed of seeing. A beautiful woman standing over him. With a dagger.

For some reason, he couldn't take his eyes off the dagger. The woman was definitely beautiful, but the blade had a design like he'd never seen. It had intricate designs etched in the hilt, and it was breathtaking. It was also massive and looked deadly. It had a serrated blade with what looked like a thumb ring by the leather handle, which could easily break another blade in two. *Why would this woman be carrying this weapon?*

He went to stand up, and she actually kicked him in the chest, and he landed back on the ground, flat of his back. "Now, hold on a minute, lady. I don't know what you're trying to pull here, but you need to step back. Don't make me arrest you because I will do it."

"I don't think so." She said through clenched teeth.

He pulled his gun out of the holster. He wasn't planning on shooting her, but she had to know who was in charge, and it wasn't her.

The last thing he saw was her smile before he blacked out.

CHAPTER 36

Chrissy had opted to ride in the back seat so Joseph Byrd could ride up front for the long drive. She had laid her head down on the armrest and was looking at Joseph. Trying to figure out if she looked anything like him.

She was also thinking of her mother and biological father and wondering if her mama was doing alright. Was she safe? Does she even remember she has a daughter?

Wondering what her biological father looked like—wondering what happened to him, how he died. She desperately wanted to ask Joseph Byrd what happened to him but hadn't been able to build up the nerve.

Allen Kensington had been her daddy. He had loved her and cared for her up until the day he went missing. He never once made her feel anything other than loved and cherished by him.

Even after she overheard the conversation between him and her Uncle James, she never repeated it, and he nor James had mentioned it to her. She had blocked what she had heard out and probably wouldn't have thought of it again if not for this situation.

So why was she thinking of her biological father now? Maybe because his actual daddy was riding in the same vehicle with her. Duh.

No matter. They needed to find out what the Quapaw have to do with stopping the evil things happening in Moon Lake. That had to come first. That and finding her mama had to be their top priorities.

Maybe she could sit down with Joseph Byrd after they put a stop to the Council. Yes, that was a good plan.

"We are around an hour from Moon Lake." She heard Henry say to Joseph Byrd. Or should she think of him as just Joseph? Yes, she needed to start thinking of him as just Joseph.

"Shhh. Let's let Chrissy sleep until we get there." She heard Joseph whisper to Henry. For some reason, that made her happy.

Chrissy felt the Tahoe come to a stop and raised up just in time to see Rose running out of the Lodge towards the Tahoe.

"Henry! Chrissy! Please get inside as quickly as possible. We have a situation at hand." She stopped at the passenger door of the Tahoe and looked almost embarrassed when she realized it wasn't Chrissy in the front seat.

"Pardon me for yelling and making a fuss." She said to Joseph as she held her hand out. "I'm Rose Hamilton. Welcome to The Lodge."

Chrissy couldn't contain her giggle when Joseph turned and smiled at her like he was used to dealing with crazy people. "Hello Mrs. Hamilton, I am Joseph Byrd. It is a pleasure to meet you."

"Please call me Rose." She said before turning to Henry. "Henry. You are needed inside rather quickly if you please."

Henry helped Chrissy out of the Tahoe then turned to follow Rose inside. "I'll see you both inside."

Chrissy looked at Joseph and shrugged her shoulders. "Let's get inside, and I'll show you to your room."

Once inside, Chrissy showed Joseph to his room then

made her way to the phone in the kitchen. She couldn't wait to hear her girls' voices.

Meanwhile, Rose motioned for Henry to follow her to the entrance to the basement. *What could she possibly have to show me that's in the basement?* Henry thought. Even though he questioned what she was doing, he still followed her down the steps. She must have a reason for taking him down there.

That's when he felt his mother's frustration like it was his own coming from the basement. He bounded down the stairs so fast he left poor Rose standing there with her mouth dropped.

"What's wrong?" He demanded before he even reached his mother's side.

Katarina briefly hugged Henry before going into the details. "I had him. Henry, I had him and let him slip out of my grip. How could I have allowed this to happen? How?"

Henry realized she was mostly talking to herself but wanted to know what she was talking about. "Who are you talking about?"

"That slimy snake, Sheriff Lucas Rollings. I caught the devil trying to rig your Jeep with a bomb! So, I brought him here to discuss things. He slipped away around an hour ago. We searched the grounds, but he has completely disappeared."

Henry shook his head. "You have got to be kidding me."

Katarina filled Henry in, starting from when she saw the sheriff watching The Lodge and ending with dragging his unconscious body down into the basement and tying him to a chair. She had misjudged his strength, or she wouldn't have left him alone for even a minute.

"Thank you for looking out for me, Mother."

"You're welcome, son. Now, how about we go upstairs so I can meet the woman who has captured your heart." Katarina said as she started up the stairs.

"Hey! About that..." Henry was trying to tell her to keep

those thoughts to herself, but she was gone before he knew it.

CHAPTER 37

C hrissy hung the phone up after leaving a message at the front desk for Anne to return her call. When she turned to leave the kitchen, she let out a gasp when she locked eyes with who she assumed was Henry's mother. At least she hoped this was Henry's mother.

Because this woman was beautiful and the exact opposite of Chrissy. This woman was blonde and petite, while Chrissy was darker skinned and almost as tall as Henry. Chrissy had no idea how exotically beautiful people found her.

Henry walked in and straight up to them, "Chrissy, this is my mother, Katarina Kesselberg. Mother, this is Chrissy Bennett."

Before Chrissy could say hello, Katarina pulled her in for a hug. "It's so good to meet you, Chrissy."

Chrissy was shocked to feel the warmth coming from Katarina. *How in the world is she warm? Aren't vampires supposed to be ice cold?* She thought to herself. Then she realized that Henry never felt ice-cold, either. Another mystery? One she was looking forward to solving, that was for sure.

"It's nice to meet you as well."

Joseph Byrd joined them, and after making introductions, Henry filled them in on what had transpired with the sheriff.

"This is bad, but time is of the essence. Henry, will you

take me to the cave?" Joseph was ready to figure out what was happening.

Geoffrey called them to the main room, and they agreed that the men would all go to the cave while the ladies stayed at The Lodge.

A short time later, Chrissy stood in the window watching as the men geared up and made their way down the driveway and to, hopefully, some answers.

Rose walked up and put her arms around Chrissy. "Honey, I know this has been a lot to take in. How are you holding up?"

Chrissy put one of her hands on top of Rose's and smiled. "Yes, this has been a lot. But, honestly, right now, the main thing on my mind is I'm missing my girls."

Katarina joined them at the window, and they all three stood there with their arms around one another for a good ten minutes.

Chrissy realized this was the closest she had felt to being a part of a family since her husband had passed. A pang of hurt for all she had lost hit her, but she tried her best to deal with it in silence. "Thank y'all so much."

She missed Dave every day, but some days it was almost unbearable. How did people do it? Get past the loss of the love of their life? Thinking of Dave caused guilt about having feelings for Henry to spread through her body. She knew he would never want her to spend her life alone, but she felt like she was betraying his memory.

The ringing phone was a great diversion, and Chrissy was thrilled to hear the girls on the other end of the line. "Mommy! We have already met Mickey Mouse and Mulan and the Fairies from Tinkerbell!" Lela sounded so excited. "I just can't wait to meet Cinderella!" Jessica put her two cents in.

"That sounds so fun! Are you girls being good for Grandma and Grandpa?"

"We are, Mommy! Grandma says we are leaving now."

"Ok, put Grandma on the phone. I love you two munch-kins!"

"We love you, Mommy!"

There had been a mix-up at the first hotel they had booked, and they had been upgraded for free, so Anne filled Chrissy in on the new hotel information. After talking through where they would be staying and contact information, Chrissy felt a peace wash over her. She always felt happy knowing her kids were safe. Those two little girls and their safety were her main priority.

Henry eased down into the cave and listened for a minute to make sure no one was nearby. They couldn't afford to have any surprises. "It's clear, but be careful coming down on the ladder." He yelled up at Geoffrey and Joseph.

A few minutes later, they were making the trek to go deeper into the cave, and when they came to a bend in the cave, Henry let them know it was a dead end. A few minutes later, they crossed the bridge then they all stopped in their tracks when they saw the waterfall. "Wow. What a beautiful sight. Such a shame it has to be hidden away in this cave." Joseph said.

They kept walking until they came upon an entrance to another room when Joseph spoke. "I sense that my ancestors were here."

Geoffrey knew he had been there before. He felt a shiver travel down his spine. "This is where the Council members wanted me to bring Rose. I have been here many times."

They got closer to an entrance to another room when they saw a warning painted outside of the entrance in his native lan-guage that read kdéde, ttą́nį sotté hi, hą́nąppáze, čʔa ttą́ka and mą́tʰe. "This has to be the cave where our Shaman kept the evil spirits locked away until he passed from this life to the next many, many moons ago. My ancestors left a warning not to enter here. The warning says there are evil spirits inside."

"Makes me want to go right in," Henry said under his breath.

Joseph lit both oil lanterns that were on the walls and looked around. The room was large, had a round table in the middle of it, but there was not much more to look at.

Even though Joseph couldn't find hard evidence the Shaman had been there, he could sense it all the way to his core.

One minute he was inspecting the walls for some clues, his head started pounding, and he fell to his knees. "Henry! Somethings happening to me!" He felt like his mind was being overtaken.

Both Henry and Geoffrey ran over and helped Joseph to one of the chairs around the table. His eyes were glazed over, and he would not respond.

CHAPTER 38

Henry looked over at Geoffrey. "Joseph is in a trance. Let's give him a few minutes and see what happens. If he doesn't wake up, we will have no choice but to call on his people for help."

Joseph was walking through a cave with a young boy. He looked at his hands and was surprised to see his hands were those of a twelve- or thirteen-year-old. *How is this possible?* He thought.

"Come on!" The other boy yelled with excitement as he waded through a stream of water that ran through the cave.

Joseph was about to walk in the stream when his friend, who Joseph knew as Running Horse, looked back at him with a look of pure fear on his face. "Something is wrong. I feel strange and want to go home."

"Let us go, then." Joseph heard himself say.

Joseph saw a white flash, and he was walking up a trail when he saw an older Running Horse with a woman on his lap. He wasn't sure why until he got closer. Running Horse was holding her limp body, sucking the life force from her body.

"Stop!" He had immediately yelled.

Running Horse threw her body down and almost floated over to Joseph. He sneered at Joseph before shoving him down the side of the mountain.

Joseph had to use all his strength to call on his spirit animal, or he wouldn't have survived the fall.

Another white flash, and then he was running through the woods. He could hear distant screams. He wasn't sure what had happened, so he kept running until the sounds of people screaming in terror were louder. He ran harder towards screams and eventually came upon a clearing with a few teepees spread out near a stream.

It was too late to help anyone when he arrived.

There were five bodies spread out on the ground, and he leaned down to see if there was any life left. He felt deep sadness when he found none.

He heard another blood-curdling scream coming from inside one of the teepees. He stepped inside, and the sight that greeted him would forever be burned in his mind.

A woman he recognized as Running Horse's mother was sitting on the floor, holding a limp body in her lap, rocking back and forth. She was covered in blood, and her face had such devastation he couldn't find words to describe it.

She turned to him and tried to speak. Her voice cracked, and after several attempts, she said, "My son." before she laid back next to the young woman she had been cradling in her arms and closed her eyes in death.

Joseph saw another white flash, and he was transported back to the cave. He opened his eyes and looked around the room before his eyes landed on his friend, Running Horse, sitting across the table from him.

Running Horse was silent, so Joseph started the conversation. "I found nothing but blood and death at our village earlier. Your mother called out for you with her last breath. Are you the one responsible?"

Running Horse smiled, and Joseph knew the thing sitting across from him was no longer his friend. "That is not what is important. What's important is what you decide for the future of your people."

"What do you want with my people?" Joseph asked the thing across from him – but it wasn't his voice. It belonged to the same young boy from the cave, only older sounding.

"I want your people to be my people. It's simple. Sacrifice the weak and old, and I will be satisfied with their offering. Refuse, and there will be consequences."

"What about my brother? He is missing, and I want him back. He has a wife that needs him!"

"Why don't you ask your brother what he wants." The thing looked over at the entrance, and another man walked in.

"Hello, brother. The Ancient One is right. Listen to him and help our people survive! He only wants those we no longer need, and he will give us great rewards in exchange. We can become immortal! Think about it. Immortal!"

Joseph looked at the man that was supposed to be his brother and remembered the story being told by his grandpa – how the evil spirit took over the Shaman's brother and turned him against their people, how one of the lesser spirits inhabited his body.

Joseph saw another white flash, and he was transported to a teepee in an Indian Village. He looked out and saw men of various backgrounds sitting around a fire talking. They were dressed like they were from a time long before.

He noticed his hands were worn and wrinkled. It seemed many years had passed since the visions started. He glanced back inside the teepee at a man he recognized as his "brother" laying on the ground tied up, then at the glowing arrowhead necklace he wore. His face twisted to one full of determination as he nudged his brother with his foot, "Brother, wake up. You will be freed of this great evil soon. I promise you."

Joseph pulled out one of the magical charms from the pouch he carried and was confident they would work. He had performed a Tribal Magic Ritual to create the charms to imprison the evil spirits. The charms looked like plain stones at first glance, but you could see they were a beautiful blue that was not a typical color for a stone upon closer inspection.

The six stones had been created as a prison for the evil spirits, and the first test would be on his "brother." He started the chant, and within a few minutes, a mist-like substance started leaving his brother's body.

His brother sat up and rubbed his head. "What happened?"

Joseph looked down at the arrowhead necklace, and it was no longer glowing, and he found himself yelling with excitement. *"They work!"*

Joseph saw another white flash and was transported back to the cave right in the middle of a battle.

White men and Quapaw Indians were fighting alongside one another. He saw four Quapaw that he knew were his sons holding up stones chanting while the white men fought with swords and knives, and other Quapaw were shooting arrows or fighting with tomahawks.

He heard a shrill laugh and knew it was the evil leader taunting him. The thing was standing near a hole in the floor of the cave. Joseph knew the time would never be better to act. He knew what he had to do, and he called on strength from his spirit animal.

As he ran, he felt his body shift and change, and he lunged at the thing, and they both went through the hole in the ground. Then, as Joseph fell, he saw his black fur and claws and realized he had transformed into his spirit animal, a bear.

He used his claws to rip open the thing's throat on the way down, and before he hit bottom, he rammed his claws in the stone wall. Then, he climbed up the wall and out of the hole.

All was calm when he reached the top. The evil spirits had been banished into the stones, and the people seemed to be bracing for another fight.

He looked down and saw human hands, then immediately started chanting. He would keep that thing imprisoned in the hole as long as possible. He only wished he could keep it imprisoned forever. But, knowing that was impossible, he decided he would leave information behind for his descendants. Information that would help them fight off the evil known as The Ancient One when the time came.

Joseph saw another white flash, and he was at the cave entrance. Boulders and rocks covered the hole so no one would easily be able to find the cave ever again. He walked to the same room and started the chant. The Magic Tribal Ritual he was chanting was meant to lock himself inside the room with the six stones containing the evil spirits. He would stay there and keep them secured as long as possible.

He saw one last flash of light before opening his eyes to Henry and Geoffrey staring at him.

CHAPTER 39

"What happened? We were beginning to worry!" Geoffrey asked.

"I was honored by being given a vision into my ancestor's past. We must continue through the cave so we can leave as quickly as possible. I will share what I learned in my vision when we return to the Lodge. First, I need to gather my thoughts."

They walked into the next area, and, on first thought, Henry assumed that it was some sort of shrine. Instead, it turned out to be a large clearing with a big hole in the ground covered with what looked like a metal rack with holes all in it.

Joseph looked around. "I was in this room for part of my vision."

Upon closer inspection, Henry realized the metal rack was a cage that was held in place by a cable that was attached to the ceiling. The line had a crank that allowed people to pull the cage up and out of the hole.

Henry looked over into the hole, and it looked like it was miles long. *What in the world?*

Geoffrey felt the blood drain from his body as memories started assaulting his mind. He flashed back to the sacrifices he had been made to watch. Back to the moment, he knew he could not allow himself to be a part of The Council. The moment he started planning his escape. He remembered a conversation he had had with his dad when he was around ten years old.

"You are going to have to toughen up, son." Arthur Hamilton said, shaking his head.

Geoffrey could still remember how his bottom lip shook with fear. "I don't understand why you all are doing this to people, Father."

"It is the way things have always been done. I need you to be strong. Make yourself of some use to Ronald. He will keep you around longer if you show yourself to be strong and willing to do what he asks...."

"What do you mean? How can I be stronger?"

Geoffrey snapped back to the present. "This is the place The Council sacrifices people. They could return any moment, and we are not prepared to defend ourselves right now. Gentlemen, we need to leave."

"I agree." Joseph seconded the idea of leaving. "After the vision, I understand what The Council members are up to. I have grown up hearing stories about a great sacrifice by evil men. I never believed these stories were fully true until today. These men are mighty, as they are not fully men, and we need to prepare before we face them. We must leave before these men return. We can discuss this further once we get back to The Lodge."

Henry felt their sense of urgency, and he quickly led the men back to the cave entrance and out into the night.

Henry went up first to make sure it was clear before they started the walk back to Henry's Jeep that they had hidden safely in the woods.

Henry couldn't shake the feeling that there were people deep in the cave. He felt the presence of at least three people, but he sensed two of them had evil intentions. But one did not.

He decided that he would come back to the cave with his mother later that night and rescue whoever was in there. He had to, or he wouldn't be able to live with himself.

As they made the trek to the Jeep, even Henry was un-aware of the pair of glowing yellow eyes that watched them as they left the cave then followed them as they drove back to The Lodge.

CHAPTER 40

Rose was in the kitchen preparing a meatloaf for dinner when she saw headlights coming down the drive. "They are back!" She yelled so Chrissy and Katarina would come to the Great Room.

She threw the meatloaf in the oven then wasted no time getting to the door so she could make sure Geoffrey was doing alright. "Honey? What happened?"

"I remember everything, Rose. Everything. And Joseph had a vision while we were there. We now have a better idea of what his Quapaw ancestors went through and how they stopped the evil spirits." Geoffrey looked as if he carried the weight of the world on his shoulders.

She couldn't help herself. She started firing questions off at Geoffrey. "Oh, honey. How bad is it? What did Joseph's ancestors do? What are we going to do?"

Geoffrey grabbed Rose's hand for comfort but also to lead her to the Great Room. Everyone else had already gathered around the table by the fireplace.

"Not only have I remembered everything about my past, but we also have more information thanks to Joseph. I'm sorry to say it is a lot worse than we could have ever imagined it would be." Geoffrey looked around the table. "It's time to lay all our cards on the table so we can figure out what is next, and please understand, we have no time to spare."

Geoffrey and Joseph then told the group everything they both learned while in the cave. First, Joseph told what his ancestors went through, and then Geoffrey shared the entire story starting at the beginning with Ronald Burgess and the other men releasing the Evil Spirits back in the late 1700s. George told them about the sacrifices, the kidnappings, how they have a Community of people that they had kidnapped over the years somewhere near Moon Lake, and he ended with how they planned on an Ultimate Sacrifice after two hundred years of sacrifices.

Katarina was dumbfounded. "So, you are telling us these men carry evil spirits inside them that ensure they age very slowly for a hundred years and that they revert to twenty-five years old at the end of their hundred-year cycle? That they have been sacrificing people for years leading up to an ultimate sacrifice that will keep them young for a supposed eternity?"

"I know this is hard to believe, but yes. That is what I am telling you."

Joseph spoke up. "Geoffrey, what you have said matches everything I have been told growing up and the vision I was gifted with during our time in the cave. All our stories that I was beginning to think were just old, made-up tales and stories we were told as children to scare us."

"If only this were a made-up tale." Rose sighed.

Joseph continued with his speech. "My grandfather always told me that our ancestors had a purpose that we can't understand. Something so much bigger than us that a Shaman from long ago gave his life to keep imprisoned. Our history tells us that there was a battle, and our Shaman's spirit was locked away. That this was for the greater good even though some bad had to come to us in these minor spirits. Do you know what he meant by this?"

"Yes, I do. Over five hundred years ago, evil reigned in this area. When a few indigenous people came together to banish the evil, they had to make many sacrifices, but they ended up working together to banish the Evil Master to a deep, dark cave far beneath the earth. It is told that a Shaman sacrificed himself and was banished with the Evil Master, also known as the Ancient One. That he chose to use all his power to travel with the Evil Master and lock him away. Unfortunately, they did not have the power or resources left over to banish the minor spirits fully, so they created the Stones to contain them. And it worked for a while. At least until Ronald Burgess and the other explorers found the Stones and released the spirits almost two hundred years ago."

"My vision showed me that the Shaman did not stay with the Ancient One after all. He changed to his spirit animal, a bear, so he could crawl out of the hole. The Shaman did sacrifice himself to keep the minor spirits locked away in the Stones. He used great Tribal Magic to keep them locked in the Stones inside that room in the cave. That is where Ronald and the other men found the Stones and released the evil spirits almost two hundred years ago."

Chrissy couldn't believe what she was hearing. "Is this all about a group of men staying young? I find that hard to believe. So what does the Evil Master or so-called Ancient One want? Do either of you know the answer to that question? I mean, what is the end game?"

"To the Council Members, this is all about a group of men staying young but also ruling in this area. Not so much to the spirits living inside them. For the Evil Spirits, this is all about releasing their master from his prison. It is about him coming back to Earth and ruling. It is about death and turmoil. None will escape him if he is released. Ensuring their master is released is their purpose and mission. Once the Ultimate Sacrifice has been completed, their mission will be fulfilled."

"This must be stopped!" Katarina was ready to fight.

"It will take planning and determination to do whatever it takes to defeat the evil spirits. First, I have to find our book of

Records that was written many moons ago detailing the same chant that the Shaman and other people who battled the evil spirits used and were able to banish them to The Stones. I must find and study this book, so we will understand how to defeat them. Then we have to find all The Stones."

"How many Stones are there?" Henry asked.

Geoffrey answered. "There are a total of six Stones. Chrissy has four here. That means we need to find the other two that are remaining."

"How are we supposed to do that?" Rose asked.

Joseph looked at Rose. "The instructions to locate The Stones are also in my book. We must get our rest tonight, and then we can make our plan tomorrow."

Henry felt he needed to tell everyone about the people in the cave. "While we were in the cave, I felt the presence of at least three people—two with evil thoughts and one with good, pure thoughts. I planned on going back tonight to investigate and try to rescue at least the one, but it's too late. So I will go tomorrow night at dark."

"Henry, I don't think you should go alone. I will go with you. I know everything I have heard tonight tells me that we must do whatever it takes to stop this evil. I am ready to fight!" Katarina knew these men were telling the truth and that this was real and happening.

Both Geoffrey and Joseph expressed their desire to help them rescue the person held prisoner at the cave, but Katarina was able to convince them the fewer people who went, the better chance they had to get in and out without being seen.

"Do you know how long we have before the Ultimate Sacrifice?" Chrissy asked.

"A little less than a month. The Ultimate Sacrifice will happen on October 31st."

CHAPTER 41

Diego Malone backed away from the window and sat down on his haunches. Shock and despair reverberated throughout his body over what he had heard. He had hoped the men he had followed from the cave would lead him to Sharon, but that wasn't the case. Not only had they not been the ones who kidnapped her, but it also looked like they were the good guys.

He thought back to the moment he found out his wife was missing. She had come to Moon Lake as a reporter for the Little Rock Times a short two weeks earlier after being assigned to follow a story about the dangers of wild animal attacks.

Her editor also asked her to check out the dam as he was curious about why there were so many tragedies there. Her main story was about the people getting lost in the massive woods and mountains that circled the area. Sharon had been happy to take the story.

She had called Diego the day she arrived in Moon Lake, which was the last time he heard her voice. He called the Econo Lodge Hotel, and they had the nerve to tell him that she had never checked in. Lies!

He had left their five-year-old son with his sister and came to Moon Lake to find Sharon. He even went to the police, and they played dumb. Like they didn't know a reporter for the Little Rock Times had been assigned a case. I told him that if she had been in town, it was likely she had fallen off the dam. Said that happened to a lot of tourists due to their negligence.

Diego knew better. His wife was not negligent and would never allow herself to fall off a dam. But, even if he believed it, what would cause the people at the Econo Lodge to lie to him? At the time, it didn't make sense.

At least he knew why now. After overhearing the conversation between the people at The Lodge, he wasn't sure what to do next. Would they allow him to help them if he offered? How would he go about the offering?

In the end, he decided to wait on saying anything. Instead, he would introduce himself to them and try to rent a room at The Lodge. That would give him time to earn their trust before telling them his story. If they said no to renting him a room, he would just have to camp out in the woods and stay on the hunt for Sharon alone.

If anyone had hurt her, they would pay dearly.

CHAPTER 42

The following day found everyone, but Chrissy gathered around one of the dining room tables. Chrissy was in the kitchen talking to the girls on the telephone. They waited patiently on Chrissy to finish checking on her girls so they could come up with a plan.

"How are the girls?" Henry asked as soon as Chrissy hung the phone up.

"They are doing well and having the time of their lives at Disney."

Joseph grabbed Chrissy's hand as she started to walk past him. "I hope I get to meet your daughters someday soon." She was surprised to see tears in his eyes.

"I hope so, too. Once we get through this, let's make it a date." She squeezed his hand and smiled.

"Something tells me there's more to the story than meets the eye with you two," Katarina observed.

"You would be correct, Katarina." Chrissy took a deep breath then told everyone all she knew about her past and how she found out that she is a descendant of the Quapaw Indians. "So, you can all imagine my surprise when I found out that Joseph here is my Paternal Grandfather."

"We are so happy for you, honey," Rose said as she got up and hugged Chrissy first, then Joseph. "Anyone else have any happy news to share with us?" She asked before sitting back down in her seat. Her eyes landed on Henry, and he felt himself squirm.

Katarina looked at Henry and shook her head yes. He felt such a relief at her approval to share their story that he almost laughed out loud. However, he realized things were too dire for him to laugh at that exact moment. "My mother and I are not like the rest of you." He started to explain when Joseph interrupted.

"Dear boy, I believe we are all aware of your situation, and there is no need for you to go through with telling us." Joseph looked at Henry then the rest of the people at the table. "Does anyone disagree?"

Henry and Katarina both smiled when one by one, everyone at the table shook their heads. Henry felt a great weight lifted. He felt almost normal. Accepted. Wanted, even.

The sound of someone coming down the drive, followed by a loud knock at the Lodge entrance, interrupted their conversation. "Goodness," Rose said. "Someone wants in! I'll be right back."

Geoffrey jumped up to go with her. "Wait for me. I don't want you opening that door without me there."

Katarina smiled at Geoffrey as he walked by her – she thought his protectiveness over Rose was sweet. However, a pang of hurt went through Katarina's heart as she thought of her late husband. No matter how much time passed, she could not forget him. He was the kindest man she had ever met, and that's why she married him. She let her mind drift back to another time and place. To a heated conversation with her father.

"Young lady, why are you so determined to ruin your life? You have your pick of suitors. So why do you choose the man with no money or connections? He works for me, for crying out loud. Why?!?"

"Because I love him! And he looks at me with love instead of greed like those other suitors! They just want your money – Karl doesn't care at all about your money – he just wants to marry ME!

Not your money!"

Katarina closed her mind to her memories when she heard Geoffrey and Rose returning. She looked up and saw they were followed by a tall, lanky man dressed in black leather pants and a matching leather jacket. She noticed that he seemed nervous by how he kept twiddling back and forth with the bandana he had pulled off his head.

"Everyone, this is Diego Malone. He comes to us from Little Rock, and he is looking to rent a room at the Lodge." Geoffrey said in the way of introductions.

Chrissy started to speak, but Rose spoke up first. "I told him we are temporarily closed due to our recent loss of your Uncle James. He was hoping the owner would make an exception for him due to his circumstances."

Chrissy couldn't help but be intrigued, so she stood up and put her hand out, "Hello, Diego. I am Chrissy Bennett. What's your story?"

Wow, Diego thought, she sure didn't waste time getting to the point.

Diego looked over at Henry and Katarina before he began talking. Hmm. He thought. They have a couple of secret weapons on their side. Maybe they did have a chance after all!

"Like Ms. Rose said, my name is Diego Malone, and I live outside of Little Rock. My wife, Sharon, works for the Little Rock Times as an Investigative Reporter. She was sent to Moon Lake a couple of weeks ago on an assignment, and I haven't heard from her since the day after she arrived here and checked into the Econo Lodge."

Chrissy felt her heart hit her stomach as she listened to his story. She could see the pain in his eyes. "I am sure you have already gone by the Hotel and to the Police?"

"Yes, and that is what makes me think that there is something strange going on here. My first stop was the Econo Lodge Hotel where she was staying, and they told me that they had never heard of my wife. Said she had never been there. Then the police told me she must have fallen off the dam due to her own negligence. They tried to tell me that this happens all the time. They said many tourists get careless, and they are never heard from again. My wife was not here as a tourist. Plus, she would never be that careless."

Henry felt the man's pain and knew it was not a ruse. He knew the man was hurting over the loss of his wife. "Did they at least file a police report?" Henry felt the hurt, but he also felt more. He felt a sliver of hope coming from the man. *Could he know more than he is letting on? That we are trying to stop the Council? Nah. He dismissed the idea.* But he knew there was more to the man's story.

"The Policeman I spoke with filed a report. Or at least he said he did, but I doubt it goes anywhere. They didn't seem to be interested in looking into her disappearance."

Henry stood up and put his hand out. "Diego, my name is Henry Kesselberg, and I am curious as to what brought you here to The Lodge. Was it just to rent a room?"

"Yes. I thought about renting a room in town but decided that might not be a good idea. I can either rent a room here or set up a camp elsewhere outside of town. I have to find my wife, and I will not leave Moon Lake until I do."

Chrissy felt her heart go out to the man. His grief was written all over his face, and she just couldn't turn him away. She looked at Rose first, "Rose, would you see about setting Mr. Malone up in one of the empty cabins?" Then she turned to Diego, "How does that sound?"

The relief he felt was written all over Diego's face and filled his voice. "I can't tell you how much I appreciate that! I will be happy to rent a cabin from you!"

Rose jumped up and headed to the front desk. "Follow me, Mr. Malone. We will get the paperwork filled out and get you checked in."

Diego nodded his head at everyone in the room before jumping up and following Rose down the hall.

Geoffrey wasn't far behind Diego. "I will take you to the cabin after Rose gets you checked in."

Chrissy smiled as Henry got up and quietly followed Geoffrey and Rose. Even though she didn't think Diego meant them any harm, she loved how he felt the need to make sure Geoffrey and Rose were protected.

CHAPTER 43

Twenty minutes later, Geoffrey, Rose, and Henry were back, and they all settled around the Fireplace in the Great Room.

"Well, that was definitely unexpected," Geoffrey said. "What do you think, Henry? Is our new friend Diego Malone being truthful about his situation and intentions to find his wife? I can't help but wonder if that is the only reason he is here."

"I did not detect any deception. So Mr. Malone is being truthful, or he is an excellent actor who also has an uncanny ability to hide his true emotions."

"I also believe Mr. Malone was truthful," Katarina added.

While everyone else was talking, Henry noticed Chrissy had picked up the phone book and was looking in the Yellow Pages. Then, a few minutes later, he heard her in the kitchen making a phone call that thoroughly impressed him.

"Sharon Malone does, in fact, work for the Little Rock Times. Unfortunately, I just confirmed that she also had not been heard from in almost two weeks. Oh, and her husband's name is Diego Malone."

"Way to go, Chrissy!" Geoffrey said.

"I think you missed your calling. You should be a detective!" Joseph added.

Katarina and Rose both hugged her and gave her a high

five.

All the fuss made Chrissy self-conscious, and she felt her cheeks burning red from all the praise. Then she looked over at Henry and felt butterflies from her head to her feet when he grabbed her hand and softly said, "I am proud of you. Great thinking."

That's probably what caused her voice to shriek when she first spoke, "So now that we have verified his story and we also know he wasn't deceptive, what are we going to do about it?"

Katarina decided to share her suspicions, "Although he was not deceptive about his wife and why he is here, he is hiding something."

"I knew it!" Rose exclaimed. "What is it he's hiding? Do you know?"

Katarina glanced at Henry to see if he shared her suspicions and was surprised when he looked just as confused as the rest of the group. "I don't know how to say this without sounding a little crazy."

"Oh, honey, I think we are good with crazy at this point," Rose stated.

"Well, then I will just say it. Diego Malone is not fully human."

"What do you mean by that?" Chrissy asked. "What is he then?" Geoffrey asked at the same time Chrissy asked her question.

"I know his kind as loup-garou, but you all will more than likely recognize either the term Lycan or Werewolf."

Chrissy was glad to hear it. Especially if he was on their side against the evil spirits. "Wow. This day just keeps getting better and better."

Rose couldn't believe her ears. "Whatever do you mean by that?"

Chrissy looked at Rose but didn't answer right away, so

Henry decided to answer for her. "I think she means that having a werewolf on our side against the Council would be a good thing."

"That is exactly what I meant." Chrissy backed up Henry's theory. "Now the question still stands. What are we going to do about it? Joseph, you have been awfully quiet. What do you think about our new friend Mr. Diego Malone?"

"I think we should get to know him and possibly even allow him to help us fight these evil spirits. He has the strongest motive of all to want to put the men of the Council down. But he will need to earn our trust first. The Great Shaman could not defeat the evil spirits alone, and he was better off once he realized that he needed help. So men from other tribes that had once been great enemies joined him and, together, they defeated the evil spirits. We should always learn from our ancestors. We don't want to repeat their mistakes if we can help it."

Geoffrey agreed with Joseph, "I vote that we keep him close as he is staying here, but we don't lay everything on him. Let's keep the details between those of us in this room. Joseph is right when he says Diego Malone will need to earn our trust. There's too much at stake."

After everyone had a say, they all agreed to allow Diego Malone to stay at the Lodge and help them in their efforts to defeat the Council and the evil spirits were the best course of action to take.

"Chrissy, would you mind if I move in one of the rooms here inside The Lodge?" Henry wanted to be close by in case he needed to protect Chrissy. Anything unexpected could happen.

"I was going to suggest that myself," Chrissy informed him.

"Now that that is settled, why don't we take a break to recharge, and we can meet back in here in an hour?" Geoffrey suggested.

"No one needs to worry about food. I have some Chicken

Salad Sandwiches made for lunch, and there is a meatloaf prepped for supper, and I am planning on making mashed potatoes and some poke salad to go with it," Rose said.

Chrissy stood up and started towards the office. "Sounds great. Rose, do you need any help in the kitchen?"

"Thank you for asking, but I have it covered. The kitchen is my happy place, you know."

Katarina found that she genuinely wanted to help. "Rose, would you mind if I helped you? It's been ages since I have cooked a meal."

"That sounds delightful. That will give us a chance to get to know one another better!"

Chrissy glanced at Henry. "I will gather up the notes Henry and I have made along with the documents and other items of evidence we have collected. By then, supper should be ready, and afterward, we can start building our plan by watching the VHS tape I have and go from there."

Katarina noticed Henry following Chrissy and smiled to herself. She was happy that he found someone he could care about. He had closed himself off from caring about his happiness for far too long, and she thought Chrissy Bennett would be the one to help him change that.

Chrissy pulled open the desk drawer in the office, looking for the few papers and the VHS tape she had left in there but couldn't find them. She was about to call for Henry when he walked into the room.

"I can't find the papers or tape. Have you seen them?" She asked.

"You put them all back in your "secret spot" before we left to take the girls to Mississippi, remember?"

Chrissy felt embarrassed for forgetting something so important. "How in the world would I forget that?"

"You have a lot on your mind. Not to mention all the crazy you have been thrown into over the past couple of months." Chrissy looked up at Henry, and he fought the urge to kiss her. "And by the way, I think you have handled yourself very well. So, you are entitled to forgetting a thing or two here or there!"

"Thank you for saying that, Henry. I am going to go grab everything from the attic." She put her hand out for Henry to grab. "Want to join me?"

He nodded, and they walked in silence, hands entwined, up to the attic.

CHAPTER 44

Lucas Rollings sighed as he walked around the cave alcove that was his prison cell. After he had gotten away from the crazy, amazing woman at The Lodge, Ronald had been furious and had him beaten and thrown deep into the cave in this cell.

Lucas hadn't known about the prison cells Ronald had designed in the unused space in the cave. There were at least five different cells. Too many secrets had been kept. *How could I have been so stupid? I allowed Ronald to take over and never once stood up and tried to stop him.* Finally, he realized it was too late for regrets as he paced the floor.

He had been talking to George Watkins, who was in a cell next to his before the simple human guard had threatened to shoot them both in the leg if they didn't shut up. If he got out of this mess, he would take pleasure in snapping that guard's neck.

He could at least still hear the Waterfall in the distance, which brought him a little peace. He was working out a plan of escape in his mind when he heard a faint sound coming from the cave entrance.

The sound was getting easier to hear as the minutes passed, and finally, he realized there were people in the cave. Lucas could only hear bits and pieces, but it sounded like they were talking about defeating the spirits and the Shaman who had created the stones. *Could it be?* He thought. *Could these people be planning on trying to beat The Council?* Good luck to them. Though, he doubted it could be done. At least not by mere humans.

He listened for a few more minutes until he heard nothing but silence. He felt a bit of relief that Ronald hadn't caught them there. But, he had to figure out a way to make the situation work out in his favor.

A plan started forming in his mind, and he smiled to himself. He would help those people defeat Ronald. He would do it and then make his escape.

Happy he had a plan; he settled in on his hard bed for the night.

Ronald Burgess slapped his flashlight a couple of times to get it turned on as he made his way into the cave. He thought back to the night he killed Bradley Whitmore and how he knew something was different but couldn't quite put his finger on it. He almost felt like a fool. Almost.

It only took him a few days to figure out what was causing his emotions to be out of whack. He had to admit he was a bit surprised when he discovered the spirit living in Bradley had entered his body after killing Bradley.

Then it took him another day or two before he found a spell to control it and all the emotions it brought to the surface.

Knowing he could not only have two spirits as part of him, but he could also learn how to control both spirits got him to thinking. Could he control three or more? How would his body feel if he had three or more spirits living with him? He could only imagine how strong it would make him!

This discovery was precisely what he needed to put the next part of his plan in place. He knew he had to do something to ensure he always held Jocelyn's love and affection, and after meeting her granddaughters, he had come up with the perfect plan!

He had started playing around with different spells, and after hours of practice and study, he could not wait to try out the latest magic he discovered on George Watkins.

If it worked out as he planned, Lucas Rollings would be next. One thing was sure; he had to act before the next Council Meeting. They were expecting to select a new Council Member, but that was not going to happen. There was no way he would be giving up the new power that flowed through his body. It felt too good, especially now that he had figured out how to control it.

He was surprised that he was met with silence when he got to the prison cells. The guard was doing his job, and Ronald appreciated a man who knew how to control others. He would have to take a closer look at the guard for a more important job later on.

He passed the cell that kept Lucas contained and kept walking without a backward glance. The now weakling that used to be a strong man was now beneath his contempt.

He started speaking the spell as soon as he walked up to George's cell, and he let out a guttural snarl when he felt the power leaving George's body and entering his own.

George was standing in the middle of the cell, looking bewildered. His arms were thrown back behind his body, his chest was raised, and his feet were raised off the ground as the spirit released him.

Once the transfer was completed, Ronald walked off as George collapsed on the cold, hard ground. George could feel every bit of energy leaving him, and he was sorry. Sorry for all the bad choices he had made over the years. Sorry for what he had allowed to happen out of selfishness. Sorry for the pain he had caused. I'm so sorry, he whispered to no one in particular as he felt the last breath leaving his body.

CHAPTER 45

Henry was thankful for the pitch black, moonless night as he and Katarina followed Ronald Burgess to the cave entrance and waited a few minutes before deciding to chance going in after him. It only took them a few seconds to travel deep in the cave where Ronald had gone before them.

They quickly discovered the area they were in was used as a dungeon. There were a few cells but only two prisoners at the time. Katarina noticed the first prisoner was all too familiar. Lucas Rollings. Ugh. He would probably give them away. She looked at him, and he shook his head and put his finger up to his mouth. *That's odd,* she thought.

They noticed a guard staring at Ronald Burgess as he chanted something they couldn't understand into the second cell.

"What is he doing?" Katarina mouthed to Henry.

Henry shrugged and quietly tiptoed towards Ronald with Katarina close behind. They needed to figure out what the man was doing. They got as close as they could without being seen, and they were both shocked at what they saw taking place.

A man was floating in the middle of the cell with a mist-looking material that wouldn't have been visible to the human eye coming out of him. Henry almost couldn't believe his eyes when he realized it was entering Ronald Burgess. But it wasn't a mist. Mists didn't have thoughts and intentions. Certainly not evil intentions.

Henry closed his mind off to everything else and concentrated on Ronald and the mist entering his body. On what he was feeling at that moment. Power. Hardcore power was flowing through Ronald, and Henry could tell he felt unstoppable.

The mist stopped, and the man hit the floor hard. Ronald didn't so much as look at him or the guard as he walked off.

Henry and Katarina hid in a slight alcove as Ronald turned towards them, walking down the corridor leading to the cave entrance. She was shocked when Lucas Rollings remained quiet. She couldn't believe he didn't give them away.

Katarina sprang into action as soon as Ronald was out of sight. She ran towards the cell and struck the guard so fast and hard he slumped on the ground. Henry followed behind her, and, together, they jerked the cell door open.

Henry could feel the remorse coming from the man and knew he regretted his decisions he had made and the life he had lived.

He also felt the man's life leaving him and knew they had mere seconds to save this man's life or let him die. The decision would have to be made quickly, or there wouldn't be one to make.

Katarina decided for them as she picked the man up and sank her teeth in his neck.

Henry should have known that would happen. He could tell that his mother had felt sorry for the man, and she did tend to act before thinking—nothing he could do about it at this point.

Katarina was already carrying the man out of the cell and down the corridor when they heard Lucas Rollings holler at them. "HEY! Don't leave me in here! I kept my mouth shut when

I could have given you away!"

They walked a bit farther when Henry stopped. "He does have a point."

"No."

"Mother…"

"No! That snake was going to kill you in cold blood. He deserves whatever he gets." She kept walking and didn't look back.

Henry followed for a few seconds before he attempted to change her mind. "He has information that we need. Plus, if we leave him here, he will tell Ronald Burgess what we did. Then we will be a target that Ronald Burgess will try to eliminate. And not only us, but everyone else at The Lodge."

That stopped her dead in her tracks. "I hate to admit it, but you are right. My only questions are, where would we take him, and who will make sure he doesn't escape?"

"I know of a cabin a few miles out in the woods on Chrissy's property. It has a fallout shelter underneath it that is secure and can be locked from the outside. We can put him down there and take turns staying in the cabin until we figure something out. I would also suggest your new friend bunking in the cabin until he has his current situation under control."

"That sounds agreeable. If you insist on taking him with us, he needs to be knocked out and tied up."

"I couldn't agree more, Mother," Henry said as he walked back down the corridor.

He walked up the bars. "Come over to the bars."

"Why? What are you going to do to me?" Henry could hear the suspicion in Lucas's voice.

"Just get over here, or I will leave you behind."

Lucas warily walked over to the bars, and Henry quickly grabbed Lucas and slammed his head into the bars. Lucas slumped to the ground and didn't make a peep. Satisfied that he was out cold, Henry jerked the bars out of their hinges and carried Lucas out of the cell and into the dark night.

The mist melted into the cave wall when Henry and Katarina got close to where it was. It sensed that those two could see it with their immortal eyes.

It was waiting patiently for them to leave so it could get down to business. It turned as it heard a noise coming from the other direction and felt a sense of satisfaction at seeing Robert Vines walking up the corridor.

He was a very gullible man, thinking he could overtake Ronald Burgess. It had put the idea in his head slowly over the past few years, and now the plan was underway.

Robert looked around and whispered. "Where are you?"

His eyes landed on the guard sprawled out on the ground, and he went over to check his pulse. He was alive but needed medical attention that he wouldn't be getting. Robert would have to leave the guard down here to die, or Ronald would ask questions. He thought it would probably take a couple of days. Oh well, the man had known the dangers of getting involved with Ronald Burgess but still did it. He had so hoped to become a chosen Council Member. That would never happen now.

The mist flew down and entered his body so they could communicate. "You have only missed Ronald Burgess by a short time." It spoke inside his head.

It could feel a shot of fear start to overtake Robert's body, so it worked to ease those fears. "Do not fear. He is gone from the cave. I would know if he was still here."

"What was Ronald doing down here?" Robert asked the mist.

"Ronald had George and Lucas as prisoners, and he was here taking over George's spirit. I watched as the mist left George's body and entered Ronald's. He is working hard to gain as much power as possible before the Ultimate Sacrifice."

"Prisoners? Can you tell me why he had them as prisoners? Has George been down here this whole time? How could Ronald possibly take over George's spirit? And where are they now?"

"Human, you ask too many questions, and none of them are the questions you should be asking."

"What do you mean by that? What questions should I be asking?"

"You will see. Just be prepared to kill Ronald Burgess on the day of the Ultimate Sacrifice."

"Are you going to be there to help me?" Robert asked.

The silence was his answer. Robert could feel that the mist had left his body, and he knew he wouldn't be getting the answers he wanted anytime soon. So he exited the way he came, so if anyone saw him, they wouldn't question why he was coming from that direction.

Especially Ronald Burgess.

CHAPTER 46

Sharon Malone looked up from her steaming cup of coffee in time to see Ronald Burgess and Jocelyn Kensington walk into the Cafeteria, hand in hand. Her stomach knotted up, but she kept a smile plastered to her face as they approached her table.

"Good morning!" Sharon cheerfully greeted them.

Jocelyn leaned down and hugged Sharon. "It's good to see you this morning. And I am so happy you are healing up nicely after your accident!"

"Good Morning, my dear. How are you feeling?" The worm Ronald Burgess said. He was such a good actor. *He probably has a shelf full of Golden Globes.* Sharon thought.

"Oh, I am doing much better. Thank you for asking Mayor Burgess." She had to play along, or she would never make it out of the so-called Community alive, much less find her sister.

Although she was beginning to think her sister was dead. She had looked everywhere for her and had not seen her. She thought about asking about her but didn't want to draw suspicion.

After she had allowed herself to be kidnapped, her captor had tied her up and beaten her. He's lucky she wanted to be kidnapped, or she would have bitten his head off his shoulders. Literally.

He said some sort of chant that she figured out was supposed to cause her to lose her memories. He then attempted to implant new memories in her brain. What he didn't realize was her brain didn't quite function like a normal human brain.

She could tell what he was trying to do, but it didn't work on her. She had played along and was still pretending almost two weeks later. She had to, or she would never find out what happened to her sister.

But this was bigger than her sister. Way bigger.

After beating her, he had brought her to a neighborhood a few miles outside of town where the people living here thought they were living in one of the only towns left in the world. They believed there was a series of natural disasters and they were "saved" by Ronald Burgess and a few other men who ran what they called the Town Council.

And Ronald Burgess was the head honcho. He was the "Mayor" of the town make-believe. What a joke. Ronald Burgess was evil. She could see it in his eyes.

Her captor had taken her to a makeshift hospital to deal with her "injuries." They were crazy. That was something she was certain of.

The Community, as she had learned they called it, the people living there had no clue they were brainwashed. They were under a spell. So far, she had discovered that The Council members were the ones who kidnapped people and brought them here to live. And she had not been able to find her sister. Anywhere. Not that she had been given many opportunities. She had noticed a guard keeping his eyes on her, so she made sure to watch her p's and q's.

She just hadn't been able to figure out why the men were kidnapping people.

What's your end game, Ronald Burgess?

The people living here thought of the town as a safe place. She thought of it as a prison.

Some people got to live in houses that were scattered around the "town," while others were forced to live in a large apartment building that looked more like a hotel.

The apartment building had rooms like a hotel and a large common area that everyone shared. It had games and a pool table to keep people occupied. Then there was the Cafeteria where three meals a day were served.

The doors were locked at night, and there were armed guards everywhere. The Residents were told that the armed guards were there for their protection. *Yeah. Right.*

Jocelyn seemed to genuinely care about people, and Sharon felt sorry that she was in the situation she was in with Ronald Burgess. She was a victim. A victim that needed help, even though she didn't realize it.

Jocelyn's voice shook her out of her fog. "Sharon, I was wondering if you would like to stop by my house and have lunch with Ronald and me today?"

Sharon swallowed down the vomit that was threatening to come up her throat. "That sounds wonderful. What time should I arrive?"

Ronald was furious. "Wake up, you incompetent fool!" He screamed at the guard.

Ronald had come back to the cave to end Lucas Rollings' miserable life. When he got to the cell, he couldn't believe his eyes when he found him missing.

Then he had discovered George's body was gone. *Who could have done this?*

Could Chrissy Bennett have been involved? She did have an immortal staying with her. But why would she have done it? He would have accused Robert or Anthony, but they had been in Florida.

He slapped the guard across the face, to no avail. Finally, he felt his pulse and realized he was near death. Oh well. That served his purposes quite well.

There had to be a sacrifice made, and he had initially planned on bringing his old secretary back with him after the Council Meeting. Now he would just use the incompetent guard. His old secretary could be part of the Ultimate Sacrifice in a few days. Either way was fine by him. As long as he could kill her, he didn't care when. He just couldn't wait to see the look of fear on her ugly face!

He glanced at his watch and realized he was running late. He grabbed the guard by his feet and started dragging him down the corridor.

CHAPTER 47

The branch slapped Chrissy in the chest so hard it knocked the breath out of her, but She didn't care. She had to keep running as fast as she could to reach her girls.

The night was so pitch black that she couldn't see her hand in front of her face. She ran by sound only. The sounds that would lead her to her girls. They needed her.

She heard Jessica cry out something she couldn't understand, then Lela whimpered, and Chrissy felt her heart slam against her ribs so hard she thought they would break into.

Reaching them was all that mattered. She had to reach them at any and all cost. They were in pain, and that hurt her soul, her core, her very being. She had to save them.

"Someone help me! They are taking my girls! Help me please!" She heard herself scream.

Her voice sounded like it was coming from a tunnel. No one answered. There was no one to help her. No one to help her girls. Except her.

That thought gave her the extra energy to push harder. To run faster. To fight and kill anyone who had hurt her babies.

Lela's whimpering was getting closer. Almost there!

Then there was nothing but silence. Chrissy spun around, grasping for anything she could hold onto. "Lela!!!! Jessica!!!! Where are y'all?"

Silence. "PLEASE!!!"

Then a scraping sound blared through the dark night. *What is that?* It was getting closer. It was getting louder.

"Please don't hurt my babies."

A sudden, bright light assaulted her eyes, and she couldn't see anything. She rubbed her eyes and blinked several times.

Finally, she saw her girls. They were on top of a Ferris Wheel, and the evil man from Aladdin was sitting with them. She ran and ran until she reached the bottom of the Ferris Wheel, only stopping in her tracks when she saw the evil man had a gun. *Please don't shoot my girls!* She tried to scream, but nothing came out – her voice was gone. She grabbed the handle on the Ferris Wheel, desperate to climb up to her girls, then he pointed the gun at her and pulled the trigger.

Chrissy screamed.

"Chrissy! Please, wake up!"

Henry gently shook Chrissy until she opened her eyes. He could only ever remember seeing one person display the amount of misery on her face—his mother after she had bitten him.

"Henry. Oh, Henry. It wasn't real?" She clung to his neck as she let her tears fall. She couldn't believe it was a dream. No, not a dream. It was a nightmare. It was her worst fears being realized in her sleep.

"Honey, it was just a dream. I heard you crying out in your sleep and got here as quickly as I could. Do you feel like talking about it?"

"I can't say it out loud. Not yet. All I know is I have to go get my girls. Now. Today. I'm booking a flight to Florida, and I am taking them somewhere far away. I'm sorry, Henry."

"I completely understand. And don't you ever apologize about putting your girls first. Do you hear?"

This is why she could allow herself to love Henry. "Thank you."

"None needed. Now, I'll let you get dressed. Then we can go fill everyone in on our plans."

"Our plans?"

"Uhm, yeah. You don't think I'm letting you out of my sight, do you? Cause I'm not."

Chrissy got ready for their trip to Florida while Henry ran out to the cabin to talk to his Mother. She was doing fine and told Henry she would stay there until they got back from Florida. He covered for her while she went hunting for a meal large enough to tide her over for a few days.

The flight to Orlando had a layover in Dallas and ended up taking them all night and through half of the next day due to engine problems with the plane. During that time, Chrissy had attempted to call the hotel from a pay phone and was told by the attendant that they were not allowed to release information about guests. They would ring the room, but no one had answered.

Henry could feel Chrissy's emotions going all over the place. She was beyond ready to see her girls. Not that he could blame her. He was excited to see them as well. He would deal with Chrissy's reluctance to allow him in their lives later. Making sure they were safe had to come first.

CHAPTER 48

Once in Orlando, they grabbed a cab and headed to the Wyndham Hotel on Chelonia Parkway.

Henry looked over at Chrissy and felt goosebumps travel up his spine when she smiled at him. *That was a first.* He thought about the goosebumps.

Chrissy had her hand on the door handle before the cab even came to a complete stop. Henry paid the driver and jumped out, running to catch up to her.

They reached the front desk at the same time, and Chrissy smiled at the attendant. "I doubt they will be here at this time, but please ring room 203."

"Of course. My name is Becky, and I'll be happy to assist. Which guest are you looking for?" The attendant asked.

"Frank and Anne Bennett."

Chrissy's smile faltered at the attendant's puzzled expression. "Is there a problem?"

"Is it possible you have the wrong room number? Frank and Anne Bennett aren't the guests in room 203."

Chrissy checked her notes. "No. That's the right room number. Room 203. See?" She showed the attendant what she had written down.

The attendant looked at her paper. "Hmm. Let me try searching by name." She started typing on her keyboard.

"Did you find them?"

"I'm sorry, but we don't have anyone staying here by that name."

Chrissy's eyes implored the attendant. "Please, check again."

The attendant looked sympathetic and typed a few more times. "They are not here. Maybe you have the wrong hotel?"

"Thank you for checking." She turned to Henry. "Let's go to my in-laws. Maybe they went home."

They took another cab, and a little over forty minutes later, they pulled into a lovely, two-story brick home in a gated community right outside of Cocoa, Florida.

Chrissy pointed at the driveway. "Their front door is open. That means they must have come home for some reason." Henry could hear the excitement in her voice.

An older gentleman who looked like Clark Gable's twin walked out the front door. "Well, hello again, Chrissy. What brings you back so soon? And who is your friend?"

Chrissy was puzzled. "So soon? I haven't been here in almost a year! Although it doesn't seem like it's been that long."

Henry put his hand out. "Hello, I'm Chrissy's friend, Henry Kesselberg."

Frank shook Henry's hand. "Hi there, Henry. It's good to meet you – the girls talked nonstop about you while they were here." He looked behind Chrissy and towards the cab. "Where are the girls?"

"What do you mean?" Henry could feel Chrissy's heart rate skyrocketing.

It was Frank's turn to look puzzled. "I mean, did you take the girls somewhere after picking them up this morning?"

Chrissy shook her head. "What do you mean? I didn't pick them up this morning." She looked over at Henry. "This can't be happening."

Frank grabbed her arm. "Come on in the house." They walked in through the foyer into a bright living area that had yellow wallpaper and white furniture throughout.

Chrissy had designed the space for them a couple of years earlier. Frank walked to the staircase and yelled for his wife. "Anne! Come downstairs, please."

Anne walked down the stairs and smiled at Chrissy and Henry. "Hi there. Henry, I didn't realize you were with Chrissy this morning."

Concern washed through Henry's entire body. *This is not good.* He thought.

"Anne," Chrissy said as she dug in her purse. "I promise you it wasn't me. Henry and I only arrived in Florida an hour ago." She pulled out her plane ticket and handed it to Anne. "Look at our arrival time."

"I don't understand. Frank, what is she saying?"

Frank turned stark white. "She's saying the girls have been kidnapped by someone who looks just like Chrissy.."

Anne's confusion was apparent. "That's not possible. You were the one who picked them up this morning. It was you! Nothing else makes sense."

Chrissy shook her head. "It was not me."

Anne screamed as if she was in agony. "No!, Chrissy, you picked them up. I promise you. It was you! I would have never allowed anyone else to take my grandbabies!"

"I believe you, Anne. It may have been someone who looked like me, but it was not me."

Frank held Anne in his arms. "Chrissy, please tell us what is going on."

"It's a long story. One that doesn't make a lot of sense, and

I don't have time to get into it right now. What's most important is for you both to tell us everything that happened this morning. Don't leave any detail out, no matter how insignificant it may seem. This will help us figure out what happened."

Anne was crying, so Frank spoke up. "We got a call from you at our hotel a little before six this morning. Or at least someone who sounded like you. You said there had been an emergency, and you needed to take the girls back to Iowa."

"What kind of emergency? And where did the person claiming to be me say I was?"

"The person claiming to be you said she had just landed in Orlando and needed to meet us at the hotel to get the girls. She didn't say for sure, just that something had happened back in Iowa that you needed to handle. She sounded quite upset, so I didn't grill her for information. I trusted that she was you."

Anne tried to talk in between sobs. "I did find it strange that this person asked for the address to the hotel. Frank reminded her that we had already given her that information, and she said she left Arkansas in such a hurry that she left the notebook with the hotel information behind on the kitchen counter."

"Anything else?"

Anne's sobs were progressively getting worse. "Yes. The girls did not want to leave with the woman claiming to be you. But she made them."

Frank sat down on the edge of the couch and put his head in his hands. "This is my fault. Anne said she had a bad feeling and I should have listened. She didn't want to let the girls go with you. But I told her we couldn't go against your wishes. Please forgive me."

"It's not your fault. There's no way you could have known this person was an imposter. It's my fault for not telling you what has been happening. I promise I will after we find the girls. You have a right to know. I can tell you this; my Uncle James stumbled upon something unbelievable and dangerous. I didn't know when I went home to Moon Lake, or I would have never gone back. I would not have taken the girls there. Ever."

Henry looked at Frank. "What was this person driving?"

"They were in a black sedan with tinted windows. Why did we let them go, Frank?" Anne walked over to the phone. "I'm calling the police."

Chrissy took the phone out of Anne's hands. "No. The police may be involved in this. Henry and I will handle finding the girls."

Frank looked at Henry then at Chrissy. "How can we know that you are really you and not the imposter?"

Chrissy looked at Frank with tears in her eyes, and she held her wrist up and showed them a gold bracelet with four small, colorful stones intertwined throughout it. "You had this bracelet specially made for me with my birthstone, Dave's birthstone, along with my parents' birthstones, and you gave it to me on my wedding day. It's not often I take it off."

Frank looked at Chrissy with pain and despair written all over his face. "Please tell us what we can do to help. We will do anything."

"Right now, I want you to go somewhere far away from Orlando where you will be safe. Somewhere you wouldn't normally go. Get out of town as quickly as possible, and don't tell anyone where you are going. Not even me."

"We can't do that. That would not be helping you find our grandbabies." Anne said between sobs.

Chrissy put her hands on both sides of Anne's face and looked her in the eyes, almost imploring her to listen. "Anne. Please do this for me. For the girls. This *is* how you can help. You know I will lay down my life to get the girls back, and we have several people ready and able to help us in Arkansas."

"Starting with me," Henry said. "I will also give my life to get the girls back if it comes down to that."

Frank looked at Anne. "Go pack a bag."

Chrissy hugged Frank first, then Anne. "Thank you, Frank. Anne, please try not to worry. I promise we will get the girls back."

Henry could feel Chrissy's emotions. They were going back and forth from fear to determination. He was proud when they landed on determination and stayed there.

She looked at Henry. "Let's go get my kids back from The Council."

CHAPTER 49

Jocelyn Kensington was giddy with excitement. Ronald had a surprise for her, and she couldn't wait to see what it was!

She spritzed her hair with a bit of Aqua Net, knowing she couldn't use much since it was her last can. But, no matter, she could live without it if she had to.

She took one last look in the mirror before leaving her bedroom and heading downstairs to meet Ronald.

He was standing at the bottom of the stairs looking happier than she had ever seen him look.

Ronald's heart stopped in his chest. "Hello, beautiful."

"Hello, Fiancé!" She pecked him on the lips. They had only been engaged a year, but she was beyond ready to marry her handsome man.

"Are you excited?"

"Very much so!" Jocelyn was hoping she would see a Preacher waiting to marry them. Now that would be a surprise! "We wouldn't be having a surprise wedding, would we?"

If only he could tell her the truth, but she would never understand that he had to wait to marry her until after the Ultimate Sacrifice. He couldn't tell her he would be required to sacrifice her if they were married. And he could never offer her up. That's where he drew the line.

Instead, for the last fifteen years, he had been wiping her

memory and making her think they had only been engaged a year. He didn't have a choice. He wouldn't have an excuse to put her off on the wedding, otherwise.

"Now, honey. You know we are planning a wedding like no other for our Community. We have to be an inspiration for our people. So many people have commented how they are looking forward to our wedding or I would marry you right now!"

Jocelyn almost felt guilty for asking. Their Community had been through so much since the world turned upside down. That's why she and Ronald had decided to have a large wedding and invite everyone. They wanted to make a big deal out of it and give everyone something to look forward to. She understood. "You're right, of course."

Ronald motioned his head towards the living area and opened the door a crack. "Don't look so down. I think you are going to be incredibly happy when you see what's in the living room."

She tried to open the door the rest of the way to peek in, but Ronald held the door firm. "Really?"

He opened the door the rest of the way and smiled at Jocelyn. "Go on. Take a look."

Sitting on the couch in the living room were two of the most beautiful little girls she had ever laid eyes on.

Chrissy looked out the window at the dark and sighed. The Pilot was preparing to land the Airplane at Adams Field Airport in Little Rock.

"Hey." Henry grabbed her hand. "We will find your girls safe and sound."

"I know we will. Ronald Burgess and the evil council he sits on must want to sacrifice them. Why else would he have taken them?"

"Maybe Lucas Rollings can tell us what Ronald plans to do. I hope my mother was able to secure him and the other gentleman, George Watkins. We are going to need her when we go rescue the girls."

"Regardless, I'm going. I can't leave the girls with that man. I have no idea what is happening, and I can't stand it. The only thing that's keeping me sane is knowing my mother is there. Maybe she's still a good person and will take care of them. If Ronald Burgess allows her to see them."

"We are all going, don't you worry about that."

"I still can't believe your mom bit George Watkins."

"Yeah. My mother tends to react before thinking, especially when she gets excited, and she was definitely excited last night. George will be a full-blown immortal in a couple of days, which will work in our favor."

"I also can't believe you rescued Lucas Rollings."

"He kept quiet even when he knew we were there, so I felt I owed him one. Plus, I was afraid if we left him behind, he would tell Ronald we were the ones who rescued George, and it would put everyone at The Lodge at risk."

"You both did the right thing."

"We did our best." Henry felt the bump when they landed. "Now, let's get off this plane and get to Moon Lake."

CHAPTER 50

Rose jumped up off the couch so fast she almost knocked Geoffrey down when they saw Henry's Jeep pulling down the driveway.

She made her way to the kitchen and got the two platters out of the refrigerator she had prepared for Henry and Chrissy earlier. Knowing how distraught Chrissy was, she figured they would not have taken the time to eat.

Plus, Henry's favorite food was rare steak, and Rose knew he would be hard-pressed to find that on an airplane.

She set the platters on the large table in the Great Room and moved back to the couch to wait on them to come in.

Geoffrey saw what she had done, and his heart was filled with love for the caring woman he married—always taking care of others. That made him love her even more, if that was even possible.

Joseph sat in a chair opposite to the chair Lucas Rollings was in. He moved his Glock-17 over to his left hand, being careful to keep it pointed at Lucas Rollings. Even though Katarina had handcuffed Lucas and tied him to a chair, he wouldn't take any chances with that one.

Chrissy gasped when she saw Lucas Rollings tied to a chair in the Great Room. After exchanging greetings and hugs, she had to find out what Lucas Rollings was doing there. "Why is he here? I thought Katarina was keeping him at the Cabin."

Geoffrey answered. "Yes, she has been. But it was time for George to learn how to properly sustain himself, so Katarina took him out to the woods to teach him how to hunt smaller animals."

Chrissy cringed. "Oh. Well, at least you have a gun on him."

They watched Chrissy disappear down the hall. "Where is she going?" Rose wondered out loud. "I made you each a platter of food."

Henry's mouth was watering already, with the pungent smell of the steak assaulting his senses. He walked over and started eating since he figured Chrissy was getting cleaned up. That is until he felt her anger hit him hard.

Chrissy marched back in the room and straight up to Lucas Rollings, putting a gun right on his temple. "WHERE DID RONALD BURGESS TAKE MY GIRLS?"

"I don't know where he took them," Lucas said calmly.

Chrissy backhanded Lucas with the butt of the gun. "Wrong answer."

"That's my girl," Joseph said under his breath. He had been wanting to do the same thing for two hours but had restrained himself.

Blood dripped down the side of his face, and he looked up at her. "I promise you. I don't know. Ronald wiped my memory of the location of The Community when he put me in that cell. I do know that Ronald said his fiancé has been bugging him about adopting a kid. I would be willing to bet that's why he took 'em."

Chrissy put the gun back on Lucas's temple. "Is there anything else?

"Yes. Ronald won't be willing to share Jocelyn with anyone, so he more than likely plans to offer them to the Ancient One."

"My girls will be offered to this so-called Ancient One over my dead body!" Chrissy felt her finger tightening on the trigger. "What are you not telling me?"

Henry gently took the gun out of Chrissy's hand. "Chrissy, he is telling the truth."

Chrissy turned on her heels and headed toward the door. "Honey, where are you going? You need to eat something."

Chrissy kept walking but at least answered Rose. "I'm going to find this so-called community, and I am bringing my girls home."

"At least let me get you something to take with you. You will need to keep your strength up. Going without eating will only hurt you and your girls." Rose scrambled to get up and almost ran to the kitchen to get a to-go bag.

"Be careful," Joseph said. "And please don't do anything until you have backup. Come back here and get us so we can go with you."

"I can't make any promises."

The gravel roads were starting to all look the same to Chrissy as they continued driving up and down every road they could find outside Moon Lake. They had used the cave as their base point and had gone every direction, hoping they would discover The Community.

Henry was thankful his Jeep had four-wheel drive, or they would have gotten stuck more than once.

"Over there!" Chrissy exclaimed. She turned to Henry. "Do you see the light?"

"I see it. Let's go check it out."

It turned out to be a couple camping close to the shore of Moon Lake.

Three hours later, they were still looking when Chrissy

spoke. "We will never find The Community like this." Henry could hear the defeat in her voice.

"Maybe not, but I know we will find the girls. I have never seen someone as determined as you, and I believe we will find them because of your strong will but mostly because of your love."

"I AM determined to find my girls. They are my life, and I will not allow anyone to take them away from me."

"I would say so. The way you hit Lucas Rollings across the head with your gun...."

"What? Did you not think I had it in me?"

"It's not that. You did surprise me, though. And did you hear what Joseph said under his breath?"

"What did he say?'

"He said, 'that's my girl."

Chrissy couldn't help but smile at that. "Wow, no, I didn't hear that."

Henry reached for Chrissy's hand and held on. Hoping she would accept the bit of comfort he was offering.

Chrissy sat there looking down at Henry's hand, holding hers, and was thankful he understood now was not the time for romance. He was simply offering her some much-needed comfort, and she appreciated it.

Her brain was working overtime, trying to come up with a way to find the Community. "Henry. Do you think Ronald Burgess grabbed my girls so he could sacrifice them?"

"Based on what Geoffrey told us about the requirement of sacrificing family members, I believe that could be the reason. At least they are most likely with your mother."

"That is true. I just wish I could be certain. I still can't believe that man is my Great Grandfather. I am just thankful it's not by blood."

"Yes. But he doesn't know that."

"That means he will bring them with him to the cave on October 31st."

"I believe it does."

"We have five days to come up with a plan on how to stop the sacrifice and save everyone, including my baby girls."

He understood what she was saying and was happy to feel hope emanating from her. "Yes!"

Henry turned around, slinging gravel everywhere as he headed back toward The Lodge.

CHAPTER 51

Diego Malone ran through the woods, his nose to the ground. He had caught Sharon's scent, and he was almost positive he would find her this time.

He had tried over and over, but he kept coming up short on finding her. Her scent would hit him, and he would search for hours with nothing to show for it: nothing but dead ends.

She had to be in the woods somewhere close. Her scent kept leading him back to the same area, but it was a dead end. Whoever had her had hidden her well. He guessed they wanted to keep their "sacrifices" safely hidden so that no one could rescue them.

According to the people at The Lodge, he only had a few days before the sacrifice to find his dear wife.

He sniffed the ground and then put his nose in the air. Nothing. He had lost her scent. Again.

Aggravated that he was doing nothing but spinning his wheels, he took off at a hard run in the other direction.

He decided that he would go back to The Lodge and offer his service. It was time to let the people at The Lodge know that he would help them fight to stop the evil in Moon Lake.

Thirty minutes later, Diego knocked on the door at the Lodge. Geoffrey answered the door and asked Diego to follow him to the kitchen.

Rose smiled when Diego came in. "Hi, Diego. You're just in time for dinner. Are you hungry? I made plenty."

"I'm not one to turn down a home-cooked meal now, Mrs. Rose. It sure does smell delicious." He had to admit the food smelled so good he was hoping for an invitation.

"Pull up a chair," Geoffrey said.

Diego looked around and noticed the lady who owned The Lodge, Chrissy, and the two immortals were missing from the group. "I believe I will." He said as he sat down. Rose filled his plate with a generous helping of spaghetti and offered for him to make his own salad. "Is the nice lady who owns this place here?"

"Why are you asking about her?" Joseph asked, almost accusatory. Diego could tell he was very protective of her.

Diego's voice shook with emotion. "To be honest, I came here to ask for your help and to also offer mine. I have searched everywhere for my wife, Sharon, and keep hitting a dead end. The police are no help, and I realize I need help."

Joseph looked at Diego hard. "What makes you think we need help, and what kind of help can you offer, Diego?

"No offense, but I think there is an evil here in Moon Lake that will take more than mere mortals to defeat. This evil has somehow kidnapped my wife and probably many other people. I am offering my unique abilities to track my superhuman strength, stamina, and desire to defeat this evil, which will only make me stronger. In return, I ask for you to include me in the plans you are making to defeat these horrible people."

Rose, Geoffrey, and Joseph all looked at Diego with wide eyes. None of them seemed to know how to answer him.

Luckily for them, Henry chose that time to join them. He searched Diego for any sign of deception and found none. Although he knew Diego had an uncanny ability to hide his emotions from Henry, he decided to go to old school. He would read his body language.

"Diego, tell us what you have uncovered so far."

"If I look at the facts, this is what I know. I know my wife came here on assignment from the Little Rock Times. She told me she was staying at the Econo Lodge, but I have since found that she did not stay there. I tracked her scent to the Homeless Shelter on the back streets of the town. So, she lied to me. I know she must have had her reasons, and I think it has to do with her sister that came up missing from this area more than twenty years ago."

Chrissy walked in. "What's going on in here?"

Henry smiled at her. "We just got a new recruit."

CHAPTER 52

Joseph Byrd used his key to unlock the box the Great Shaman had left behind. The box held items their ancestors had held as sacred. His family had kept these items locked away in the container for many generations, and Joseph had left it all there once it was passed down to him.

Both the box and the book had been passed down and kept safe for generations. Until around a hundred years ago, the men stopped looking at The Old Book of Records as sacred. They had packed it away and had not given much thought to it since then. When Joseph inherited it, he had placed it in a place of prominence in his home.

He removed the book and paused when he picked up the box to move it. It just felt too heavy to be an empty box. He looked inside and then measured the box. *Hmmm. There has to be something else in here.*

He knocked on the bottom of the inside of the box a few times before pushing on the corner. Pop! The bottom clicked out, and two small pouches were hidden inside the bottom of the box. Inside each pouch was an arrowhead attached to a long strip of leather.

He knew the arrowhead necklaces were significant but couldn't put his finger on why. He tried to remember, but nothing surfaced.

He picked up The Old Book and held 3it close to his heart,

then carefully looked through the pages for the chant that would rid their world of the evil spirits.

He smiled to himself when he found the page he was looking for and began reading the text he was convinced would save them.

As he headed to the Great Room to practice the chant on Lucas Rollings, he remembered the vision when he was in the teepee with his "brother." He remembered how he was wearing an arrowhead necklace that glowed before the evil spirit was banished to the Stone.

Rose waved at him as she was at the end of the hall, so he filled her in. "Rose, I have to go back to my room to grab something. I will be right there." He then quickly turned around to retrieve one of the arrowhead necklaces to test his theory.

Katarina glanced over at Lucas Rollings, who quickly closed his eyes and pretended to be asleep on the pallet Rose had made him by the fireplace. Geoffrey had hooked a chain to the fireplace and handcuffed Lucas to it to keep him from escaping.

"Stop staring at me."

"I'm not staring at you." He lied.

"Liar. I don't know what you're planning, but you better get it out of your head. Because I **will** hurt you."

Lucas couldn't help it; he was utterly fascinated by Katarina. He rubbed the gash on his temple and chuckled. "I take it most of the women in this house have no qualms about hurting people."

Katarina stood up and started walking toward where Lucas was lying on the floor by the fireplace. "Stop talking, or I promise you I will..."

Henry and Chrissy walked in, interrupting what Katarina was saying. "Mom. We have a plan, and we need to talk to everyone." Henry looked around the room. "Where are they?"

"Headed this way!" Rose said as she walked in, followed by both Geoffrey and George. "Joseph said he needed a few minutes to run back to his room to grab something."

Chrissy yawned. "That will give me time to grab a cup of desperately needed coffee."

Rose followed Chrissy to the kitchen. "How are you holding up, honey?"

"I feel like I am living in the middle of my worst nightmare. All my fears are hitting me at once, Rose, and the only thing keeping me going is the thought of bringing my girls and mother home."

"I know we will bring them home." Rose hugged Chrissy, wishing she could somehow help Chrissy find a way to release the emotions built up inside.

A few minutes later, everyone besides Joseph was gathered around the table in the Great Room, trying to decide what to do with Lucas Rollings while they met.

Joseph walked into the room, and the first thing Chrissy noticed was a glowing arrowhead necklace around his neck.

"That's new." Chrissy commented.

"Yes, it is. I found this with The Old Book our ancestors left for us. I recognized the arrowhead from my vision. Chrissy, will you please bring one of the Stones to me? I want to try something."

"I have them in my bag." She grabbed her bag and handed Joseph the entire pouch that contained the Stones.

Joseph removed one Stone and started walking toward Lucas. Rose was surprised to see it was almost glowing a beautiful blue color. Joseph held the Stone up high and started chanting old Quapaw words:

i-ki-shi-ke wa-na-xe di-e e-ti **da** ko-zhi hi ni-ka-shi-ka de-do ki-we i^n-ch^{h}o^n

Lucas turned white as a sheet. Joseph repeated the chant:

i-ki-shi-ke wa-na-xe di-e e-ti **da** ko-zhi hi ni-ka-shi-ka de-do ki-we i^n-ch^{h}o^n

Both Henry and Katarina could see a faint mist that looked like a halo moving around Lucas's entire body. It looked like it was attempting to fight off what Joseph was doing, but it struggled to maintain control.

"Whatever you're doing, it's working!" Henry couldn't keep the awe out of his voice.

Joseph's voice grew stronger and louder as he continued the chant:

i-ki-shi-ke wa-na-xe di-e e-ti da ko-zhi hi ni-ka-shi-ka de-do ki-we i^n-ch^{h}o^n

i-ki-shi-ke wa-na-xe di-e e-ti da ko-zhi hi ni-ka-shi-ka de-do ki-we i^n-ch^{h}o^n

Joseph held the Stone higher, beckoning the evil spirit to enter. He repeated the chant several more times before he was able to overpower the evil spirit and banish it to the Stone.

Everyone watched Lucas's body shake as the mist left his body. Only Henry and Katarina could see the mist as it left Lucas and entered the Stone, but they all could tell it was happening.

Lucas's lifeless body hit the floor, and Joseph turned to him, chanting more words in the Quapaw language:

jhi-e shi-no^n kjhi ki-ta gi-ta
jhi-e shi-no^n kjhi ki-ta gi-ta

After Joseph repeated the chant a few more times, the stone had turned a glowing red. Lucas blinked his eyes and tried to stand up, not realizing he was handcuffed to the fireplace. He slammed down rather quickly and looked around with a confused expression on his face.

George Watkins looked at Katarina and winked. "Where was this man when we needed him?"

Lucas let out a welp when he saw his leg handcuffed to a chain that was secured to the fireplace. "What just happened? Why am I handcuffed? What have you people done to me?" His lower lip trembled, giving away how scared he was.

He looked so scared that Katarina almost felt sorry for him. Almost but not quite. "You are a very evil man, and we have you handcuffed to prevent you from running off and hurting anyone else. Are you trying to say you don't remember who you are or what happened?"

Joseph turned to Katarina. "He should regain his memory in a few days, but for now, he will not be able to recall anything."

Katarina was skeptical at first but didn't detect any dishonesty coming from Lucas, so she decided to give him a break.

"Look. I apologize for being so rude. Just know you are here partially for your protection. That's all I will say about it."

"Will you at least take the handcuffs off?"

"No. You would just try to run away."

"I can't imagine ever trying to run away from a woman as beautiful as you."

Henry winced. "Okay. That's enough. You lay back and get some rest." Lucas tried to interrupt, but Henry held his hand up. "You will not be harmed. I give you my word."

Lucas laid back on his pallet but kept his eyes on the group of people who had him held prisoner.

Everyone else in the room looked at Joseph as he collapsed

in the recliner and closed his eyes. After a few seconds, he opened his eyes, and they landed on Chrissy.

"What was that?" she asked.

"The boxes I brought with me contained items that our people have had for many moons. Items that have been packed away and forgotten for a long time. I brought them with me because, after our conversation in Quapaw, I remembered part of the stories from my childhood. Legend says that our Shaman wrote down the steps to banish evil spirits. He did this because he wanted his descendants to be able to protect themselves."

Joseph motioned over to Lucas. "When I found the Old Book of Records, I knew I needed to test it on the man here before attempting it on the rest of the Council."

"Well, it worked." George Watkins said. "I can tell that by how the Stone changed from blue to red."

"Indeed." Geoffrey agreed with George.

"What next? How and when do we get the rest of the evil spirits banished?" Rose asked the group.

"We have a few days until the sacrifice. We must practice building our strength, but we also must get plenty of rest to renew our bodies. We must also plan out every move we will make. We must also find the other two Stones."

"May I see the Stone you just used, Joseph?" Katarina asked, and she inspected it for a couple of seconds. "I know where the other two are."

"What? Where?" Rose asked in disbelief. "You are fast!"

"I saw them when I was visiting the Mayor's office. Henry, you, and I should go get them now. They are on the bookcase in plain sight."

"I agree that you two should go. You can get in and out the quickest." Chrissy answered.

"I suggest we take a break until Henry and Katarina return," Geoffrey said.

They all agreed to take a mental break to be prepared when it was time to start using their physical strength.

CHAPTER 53

Chrissy stood at her bedroom window and stared at the lake. She knew she needed a way to release her pent-up anger, fear, and frustration. She was terrified of losing her girls for good, and she needed to gain control of her emotions so she would be of some use when working to stop The Council.

The glistening lake seemed to beckon her, and within minutes she was out the door running down the dock, stripping her bathing suit cover off. She dove in the water and swam as far as she could towards the bottom. She had to be strong for her girls. She couldn't lose her mind. Not now. Too much had happened since her uncle had died. Too much, too fast.

Chrissy stayed underwater as long as possible, driving herself to the brink of drowning before coming up for air. She needed that release to help her focus and get her mind straight.

She had been dealing well, though. Up until her girls got took. That was something she couldn't deal with – feeling like a failure as a mother. Doing what she thought was right only to find out it was the wrong thing after all.

She swam until her muscles ached before she decided to swim to the dock. She didn't feel good, but she at least felt ready to tackle what was ahead. She was prepared to fight to the death to save her baby girls. She could feel the determination in her bones, and she was glad. She knew that is what it would take to bring her girls home.

Once she surfaced, she saw Rose sitting on a bench on the dock holding a towel. "Hi, honey. I won't ask if you are ok because I already know the answer to that question."

Chrissy climbed out of the water and gratefully took the towel. "Thanks. I didn't even think to grab a towel." She stared out at the dark water. "Rose, I am not ok, but I am determined. I'm determined, and I am ready to do whatever it takes to bring my girls home."

A chill traveled down Chrissy's body, and she knew it was more than the cold October night causing it. She longed for days when the cold wind was all she had to worry about.

Robert Vines sat down at the large rock table and looked over at Anthony Hightower. "Do you have any idea why Ronald, George, and Lucas are late?"

"No telling. Somebody probably made Ronald mad again."

They both almost jumped out of their skin when they heard someone coming down the corridor. "I need some help out here," Ronald yelled from outside the room.

Both men jumped up and headed out the door to see what Ronald was yelling about. Anthony was shocked to see Ronald dragging one of their guards by his feet. Robert, not so much since he already knew the guard was nearing death from the day before.

"What did you do to him, Ronald?" Anthony asked, almost in disbelief.

"Anthony, grab one of his legs, and Robert, grab the other." Both men grabbed a leg, and they made their way to the Offering place.

Robert and Anthony were both silent as they carried the unconscious guard.

Ronald broke the silence. "I found him like this. Someone else did this to him, and I figured we could go ahead and use him as the sacrifice this time instead of old what's her name."

Anthony grunted with the weight of the guard. "Who could have done this? It's not like people know we are down here."

"I wonder where Lucas and George are." Robert wondered out loud. He wanted to see if Ronald would come clean and tell them the truth.

Ronald let out a sound of disgust. "Those traitors are incapacitated."

Anthony and Robert looked at one another. "What do you mean by traitors?" Anthony asked.

Ronald's lips curled back in a cruel smile. "They were trying to take over the Council. Wanted to overthrow everything we have worked so hard for. So, I took care of them. It's not like they gave me much choice."

Robert felt such a sense of relief that Ronald thought Lucas and George were the traitors he wanted to jump up and down. He somehow managed to contain his emotions, so he didn't give himself away. "What makes you think that? Those men have been part of The Council for years. Are you sure they are traitors?" He tried his best to sound sincere.

He didn't bank on making Ronald mad. "Yes, I'm sure, you idiot! Do you think I would accuse two of my best friends of doing something this grave if I had doubts?"

"Of course, you are right, Ronald. Forget I asked."

Ronald looked at Anthony to make sure he wasn't about to challenge him as Robert did. "You got anything to add or ask about my decision-making ability?"

"Sure don't. If you say Lucas and George are traitors, then they are traitors. I know you well enough to know you wouldn't throw out false accusations. You have proof, and I don't need to see it. I trust you, Ronald." Anthony truly meant what he said.

Robert threw up a little in his mouth. What a suck-up. *I trust you, Ronald.* Anthony didn't know it, but he had just picked the side he was on when it was time for the showdown. The wrong side.

Once in the Offering Room, they pulled up the metal cage and threw the guard's lifeless body inside. Ronald cranked the motor and lowered the cage.

Ronald couldn't decide if he was going to let Anthony and Robert live on our not. He needed support, but did he need more immortals getting in his way? He already had three spirits residing inside him. He felt that he could take on a few more and still maintain control. He was strong enough.

It was almost surreal to Ronald that this would be the last single sacrifice they would have to make. The Ultimate Sacrifice would be held in a few days, and after that, Ronald would be able to live forever. Forever with his love, Jocelyn. They would be able to do anything they wanted. To have anything they wanted. He could not wait.

He planned on having their wedding immediately after the Ultimate Sacrifice was completed. They would be married in the cave right by the waterfall. It would be a beautiful wedding, and she would be so surprised!

The tingle in his blood alerting him that one of the Stones was activated was not expected or wanted. He knew George was dead but wondered if somehow Lucas was involved. He had to be. What could he be trying to do? Whatever it was, he would not be successful at it. He felt regret for not killing Lucas when he had the chance hit hard. He would remedy that mistake the next time they met.

CHAPTER 54

"It's my turn to practice with Katarina." Lucas said as he watched Katarina and George spar. He wasn't surprised to feel a pang of jealousy hit him.

Katarina looked at Lucas with disdain when she sensed what he was feeling, "Really?"

Lucas smiled sheepishly. "I can't help it. And you need to quit that. It's not fair."

"Get over here and I'll show you what's not fair."

"You're gonna practice with me?" Lucas couldn't believe his ears.

"Hurry before I change my mind."

George smiled at Diego, "I guess it's you and me."

"I'll stay in my human form so I don't hurt you too badly." Diego teased.

"Alright then. I appreciate you for being so considerate." George laughed.

Henry kept an eye on his mom and Lucas as he and Chrissy attempted to spar. They were out by the old cabin in a clearing that was perfect for practicing. Has plenty of room for combat and Rose had set up a table with snacks and drinks.

Henry could tell that Chrissy didn't want to try to hit him and he thought it was adorable. "Come on, take a swing. Don't be scared!"

He was rewarded with a jab to his side. "Ok ok that's better. Now, Im gonna come at you and I want you to try to block me."

Chrissy groaned, "I thought I was in charge of banishing the spirits to the stones with Joseph and that you would be protecting me. Shouldn't I focus on that instead of fighting?"

"What if something happens to me? You need to be prepared for every possible scenario."

"Listen to Henry, Chrissy. He is right in what he's telling you." Joseph agreed.

"I know. I'm sorry. Come on then Try to hit me!"

Henry walked up with his hand out like he was offering to shake her hand then he suddenly changed course and went toward Chrissys face. Smack! Chrissy slapped his hand away before he reached her face. He was impressed. Once again. "Great job. Let's go again."

Chrissy looked over at the cabin and sighed. Her bones were weary and her muscles ached but she had to keep going. They would be at this for the next few days and she was fine with that. As long as she had enough strength left to bring her family home. That's all that she could hope for.

"Y'all are doing so good." Rose had been there the whole time cheering them on.

Chrissy looked around at everyone as they practiced and was grateful. Grateful they were on her side. She knew she couldn't have handpicked a better group even if she tried.

"Can I have everyone's attention for a minute?" Chrissy shouted over the fighting. "I want you all to know how much I appreciate what you're doing. I'm thankful for each one of you and wanted you all to know that. What you're doing for me and my girls can never be repaid."

"We would never ask you to repay anything." Katarina spoke first.

Geoffrey and Rose raised their intertwined hands, "We

love you and your girls and we are willing to do whatever it takes to stop the evil within Moon Lake." Rose said.

"I look at us like a crime fighting, evil stopping, innocent saving team." Diego winked at Rose and she actually blushed.

Then George spoke up. "I have to do this. You know kinda like righting the wrong and I suspect Lucas feels the same way."

"Yes. One hundred percent even though I know there's nothing I can ever do to truly make things right. But I plan on spending my life trying." Lucas agreed.

Diego put his arm out and signaled everyone to place their hands on top of one another. After they were in a circle, hands all on top of one another he yelled out, "we can do this, team! Let's take down the Council and make Moon Lake a safe place!"

"Team!" Everyone yelled out.

Katarina looked at Henry and smiled at the hope they could both feel emanating from the group of people, once strangers now turned friends. Friends fighting for the same cause.

CHAPTER 55

The day had arrived. Halloween. October 31. The day they would either stop Ronald Burgess or die trying.

Chrissy walked into the Great Room and found Lucas Rollings sound asleep with George Watkins sitting in the recliner watching him like a hawk.

"Morning, George." Chrissy wondered if he wanted to drink her blood then quickly dashed the thought. Katarina and Henry had worked with George on the type of blood he was to drink, which was only animal blood. Human blood would drive him mad, and he would end up a Rogue Vampire. She sure hoped that didn't happen with George.

He greeted her without taking his eyes off Lucas. "Good morning."

"How about I relieve you for a bit?"

"I would say no, but Katarina tells me that you can take care of yourself. So, I will take you up on your offer. I'll be back within thirty minutes."

"Take your time."

She waited until she heard the front door shut. "I know you're awake. So quit faking."

"Man, you are good. How could you tell?"

"I'm a mom. Why were you pretending to be asleep?"

"Because that man is crazy. He has been staring at me nonstop all night long. I know he wants to hurt me for some reason. Hey, can you please go find Kat for me? I need to talk to her."

"Kat?!?"

"Sorry. Katarina."

"She will be back soon. What do you want with her?"

"I regained my memory."

Chrissy wasted no time running into the kitchen. "Henry!"

Henry stepped out of the kitchen, and they collided. "Whoa!"

"We have to find your mom. Lucas has his memory back, and he wants to see her."

Henry didn't care for the obvious attachment Lucas had for his mother. But he would deal with that later.

"She's hunting, but I will go get her."

A few minutes later, everyone gathered in the Living Room, including Diego.

When Lucas first started speaking, he kept his eyes cast downward. "First things first. I owe you all an apology. I have been involved in many evil schemes over the years, and not once did I try to change. I allowed myself to beat and kill people, to do things that are unspeakable."

He looked up and met everyone's eyes before continuing. "Words cannot express my sorrow. My regret. My pain. I deserve death and nothing less. I am sorry for what I have done, and I give each of you my word that I will help you defeat Ronald Burgess. IF you will allow me to."

No one said anything, so Lucas continued. "Ronald plans on sacrificing one hundred people tonight. Once this is done, it will release terror on this world like no other. The gates will be opened for all types of evil to enter. In payment, Ronald and the other Council Members will be allowed to live for all time with whomever they desire."

Lucas looked at Chrissy. "And Ronald desires your mother. He has kept her living in The Community for right at fifteen years waiting to marry her after the Ultimate Sacrifice is completed tonight."

Chrissy felt nauseous at the thought of her mother marrying Ronald Burgess. A man she had only seen in photos but still despised with her entire being.

"Why is he waiting to marry my mother?"

"Ronald was too smart to marry her before tonight – he knew he would have had to sacrifice her if they were married, and he would not ever do that. Your mother is the only person that man has ever genuinely loved."

A sudden dread hit Chrissy at the core. "What about my children? I hate to think that he is truly capable of killing them."

"He has done it to many other children in the past, including his own, and will have no problem doing it again tonight with your girls. It's imperative we stop him."

"We?!?" Katarina shrieked. "You are not helping us!"

"Why? Because I was one of them?" Lucas implored Katarina with his eyes. "I *was* one of them, but I am not anymore. Yes, I did everything I could to help Ronald. But I promise every one of you I am not that person anymore. I am sorry for what I have done. So deeply sorry. And I need to help. I will do anything to help stop Ronald and the rest of the Council members. ANYTHING!"

Henry knew the remorse Lucas displayed was no act. He could feel the sorrow and regret coming from Lucas like a huge ocean wave slapping him in the face.

Henry looked at his mom. "I vote we allow him to help."

Joseph agreed. "We can use the help. Katarina, the chant I performed, removed the evil spirit from Lucas. The man standing here now is not the man who stood there a few days ago."

Everyone else in the room agreed that Lucas should be allowed to help.

Katarina narrowed her eyes. "Fine. But if you make one false move, I will slit your throat."

Lucas grinned at her. "I would expect nothing less."

CHAPTER 56

Brenda Vines peeked around the door and saw her husband, Robert reading the Little Rock Times at the kitchen table. She grinned to herself and tippy-toed into the kitchen, doing her best to be as quiet as a mouse.

"Boo!!!" She screamed out at her husband from behind the pantry, and he knocked his coffee over, trying to get away from her.

"Brenda!" Robert was red-faced. He couldn't believe she had caught him off guard! His mind had been wandering to the upcoming sacrifice and his plans to overthrow Ronald. He was already a bucket of nerves, and Brenda scaring him didn't make it any better.

"Why did you do that?!? You made me spill my coffee! You know I am on my way to meet the Mayor and need to look my best. I will be helping him, and a few more gentlemen get the cave set up for the surprise wedding."

She looked at him and couldn't stop the giggle that escaped. "I'm sorry, honey. I was just playing around. You know I like to mess with you."

He couldn't stay mad at her for long. Especially knowing what tonight would bring. Sadness hit him over the thought of losing her, but he knew there was no getting around it. He shouldn't have ever married her. He had been selfish.

Ronald had been smart by not marrying Jocelyn. A wave of jealousy hit him at the core. He hated that Ronald had always stayed a step ahead. Making him and the other Council members look bad.

Robert had felt such an intense love for Brenda that he hadn't thought things through. He wanted to marry her, and he had.

It had been love at first sight when he saw Brenda. She and that little weasel of a boyfriend she had at the time were kidnapped and brought to The Community around twenty years ago, and he had been smitten.

She was at least twenty years his junior when they met, and he didn't think he would have a chance with her, but she had surprised him. She had turned to Robert for comfort after her boyfriend "ran away," and eventually, she ended up loving him back. Of course, she would have hated Robert if she had known her boyfriend had been sacrificed at his request.

He had a few secrets he kept from her, for her good and his. Their son not dying when he was a baby was one of them. That was something she would go to her grave, not knowing.

Sharon was on high alert. Something was going on with the men who ran the "town." They were gathering people up, and she couldn't figure out why.

She looked up from the book she was pretending to read when Ronald Burgess approached her. "Hi, Sharon. I'm inviting Jocelyn's favorite people to a surprise wedding I am having for her tonight, and I know she would not want you excluded. She just thinks the world of you."

Sharon watched Ronald's eyes darting all over the place, and she knew he was not being sincere. "Really? A surprise wedding? How are you pulling that off?" She forced a smile to her face.

"I've been planning this for an exceptionally long time and have had plenty of help. We will surprise her at a cave I found on the outskirts of town – it has the most beautiful waterfall you could ever see, and she will go crazy over it. Are you in?"

Yes, of course, I am in, you liar. Sharon thought before giving him a more appropriate answer. "Oh, yes. I wouldn't miss this surprise wedding for anything in the world!"

Ronald could feel the spirits inside him getting antsy. They were ready to complete the sacrifices so their Master would be released from his prison.

What they didn't know was Ronald planned on overtaking their Master. Ronald already had three spirits living inside him, and he had no problem controlling them. So why bow down to the Ancient One when he should be the one running things?

He planned to allow Robert and Anthony to live with their measly one spirit while Ronald kept the three spirits he had plus the Ancient One. He was ready to have that power!

He smiled as Evelyn, the town's beautician, came running over to him. "Mayor! I can't wait to see the look on Jocelyn's face tonight! Oh, this is so exciting!" Evelyn batted her eyes up at Ronald. "Jocelyn is such a lucky woman to have you."

"Now, Evelyn. If I didn't know any better, I would think you were flirting with me. You know Jocelyn would get ahold of you!" He said jokingly.

"It's hard not to flirt with the best-looking man in town, Mayor. But don't you worry, I know you are taken! I'll see you tonight – I have an appointment coming to get their hair done for your big event!"

Ronald watched her walk back into her beauty shop before continuing on his way. He was in good spirits thinking of the night ahead.

CHAPTER 57

Chrissy pulled her hair back in a ponytail and attempted to braid it when someone knocked on her bedroom door. "Chrissy, it's Katarina. I have something for you."

"Come on in, Katarina!"

Katarina walked in and handed Chrissy a black outfit. "I made this for you. It's exactly like mine."

Chrissy looked at Katarina's outfit and saw that it was also black. "It's made from a comfortable material that will move with you. Very functional for what we will be doing tonight."

Chrissy was touched. "I don't know what to say. Thank you for thinking of this."

"No problem." Katarina smiled. "It's kind of what I do. Making sure everyone has matching outfits. You know, I want to help out where I can."

"Seriously? How in the world have you had time? And you have helped out more than you know."

Katarina laughed. "I have had plenty of time. You know, all night every night while everyone else slept."

"Oh." Chrissy's mouth formed a solid O.

Chrissy stepped into the bathroom and changed – she wasn't surprised that it fit perfectly.

"You are really good – this fits me like a second skin!"

"Thanks! Now turn around and let me do something with your hair to keep it up all night."

Chrissy turned around, and Katarina continued talking. "I have noticed the way you and my son look at one another."

"Um. Um." Chrissy stammered.

"I know now is not the time to get into this, but I want you to know that I approve. Wholeheartedly."

"Oh. Um. Thank you."

"There. Your hair should hold up all night long." Katarina had French braided Chrissy's hair, then secured the bottom in a bun.

"Wow. That looks and feels great. Thank you, again."

"You're welcome. Now let's get everyone else and go kick the Council's tails!"

Henry noticed Chrissy twirling the arrowhead necklace around her finger as she looked out the window of his Jeep. Lucas, Rose, and Geoffrey were in the back seat, discussing how they would work together to save as many people as possible.

Katarina, George, and Diego had opted to travel to the cave on foot.

Chrissy felt like she was going to throw up. But she couldn't. Her girls depended on her, and she would lose her own life before letting them down. *You can do this. Just remember what Joseph taught you.*

She repeated the chant over and over in her head to make sure she still had it down. She then felt in the velvet pouch for the Stones and let out a sigh of relief. The Stones were there. Not that she thought they wouldn't be there. She had just packed them before they left. *Remain calm, Chrissy.* She told herself again.

Henry reached over and squeezed her hand. "I believe in

you. You know that chant better than you know your own name. You will be able to banish any evil spirit that you see. I know you can. Just remember our plan."

"I know. I'm just worried about my girls. And my mom."

"We will do everything in our power to bring not only your girls and mom out but everyone," Geoffrey said.

They had a solid plan. Lucas and Geoffrey would work on getting everyone out of the cave. Rose would stay outside the cave to direct everyone to safety while the rest would find the Council Members and stop their plan.

Yep, the plan was solid. Chrissy just hoped everything went off without a hitch.

CHAPTER 58

Ronald looked around at the people laughing and talking over by the waterfall. They were all so clueless. They were so easily led and had come to the cave to meet their death by their own free will.

They hadn't even noticed that Jocelyn wasn't there for her own "wedding." She was at home, hopefully sleeping like a baby for now.

He had one of the guards watching his house, and he had been instructed to bring them at 2:00 a.m. Family members had to be part of the last wave of sacrifices, and Ronald felt like he was being generous by giving Jocelyn a little more time with them.

It was almost midnight—time for them to get started. "Anthony, Robert, meet me in the Offering Room. We need to get the first wave ready."

Ronald had put a spell on fifty military men from the Air Force Base in Jacksonville, and they were there, ready to assist with the Ultimate Sacrifice.

Ronald walked into the Offering Room and could feel the energy all around. It was almost time. He was giddy with excitement as Anthony and Robert walked in with five men from The Community.

◆ ◆ ◆

The mist that was the Ancient One was right at the edge of the hole. It could feel Ronald's excitement like it was its own. It only needed another sacrifice, and it would be free. Free to take on its human form outside of its prison. It couldn't wait to look Ronald in the eye and end his miserable life. To see the look on Ronald's face was something the mist had envisioned for many years.

Robert felt the Ancient One losing patience with him. He had to do it. He looked at Ronald and Anthony as they were preparing to start the ritual, and he grabbed one of the offerings and pushed him down the hole, to his death and the freedom for the Ancient One. Robert then repeated the chant he had been practicing causing everyone in the room to become like statues. Everyone but himself and Ronald. He couldn't have the people trying to kill him after he stabbed Ronald. They were loyal to the sorry excuse for a man.

Ronald had a look of confusion on his face. "Robert, what in the world have you done?"

Robert looked at Ronald with a firm resolve and remained silent, not wanting his voice to give anything away. He had to stab him right by his heart. Close enough to maim him but not kill him. He would do it so he would be weak when the Ancient One confronted him.

He pulled out his knife and took off at a dead run with Ronald in his sights.

They had walked in on a party. People were laughing and having a good time like they didn't have a care in the world. Chrissy was a little thankful since they were able to blend in easily. No one had given them a second look.

She looked at Henry with a confused expression on her face.

Henry leaned over and whispered. "Remember, they had

to get the people down here, and a wedding was the easiest way. These people have no idea Ronald brought them down here to be sacrificed."

"Sharon's here! I can feel her!" Diego exclaimed. "I'll be right back. I have to find her."

Sharon looked up when she caught a whiff of Diego. She couldn't believe he was here. Then he was standing right in front of her, kissing her face. "I have been searching all over for you!"

Sharon kissed him back. "I have so much to tell you. These people are crazy, D. I mean crazy."

"I know. I'm here with a group of people to stop The Council. Oh, and three of them are Immortal."

"Immortal?!? Ok. What are y'all stopping? The wedding?"

"Sharon. The Council brought you all down here to sacrifice you to evil spirits." At her look of disbelief, he looked her in the eyes. "It's a very long story, but we need you. We need your help. These people need your help. Trust me?"

"I trust you with my life, but that is kind of crazy sounding, D. I came here to find my sister and have found more than I bargained for. Even so, the idea of evil spirits is a stretch."

"Please trust me. The future of our world depends on it."

"That is deep, D. But you know I am with you. Always. After this is all over, you can explain." She walked up to the group with him, and Diego made quick introductions.

"This way." George motioned them with his head to follow him down the path on the right.

Chrissy tried to control her breathing by practicing breathing techniques to help herself remain calm. She felt in the velvet pouch again to make sure the Stones hadn't magically disappeared. They hadn't.

Joseph grabbed her hand. "You are a descendant of the Shaman who built these Stones, who initially banished these evil spirits. You have Quapaw blood flowing through your veins.

You are a warrior at heart, and you can do whatever you put your mind to."

Joseph had said those words to her many times during their training. She knew it. But right now. This moment. She needed to hear them. Again. She reached up and kissed his cheek. "Thank you."

Henry smiled as he felt some of the terror leave Chrissy. He knew she was fearful, but she was motivated to overcome that fear. Motivated by love.

George had disappeared into another room and was back within ten seconds. He put his finger to his mouth, signaling them to be quiet. Chrissy almost couldn't hear what he said. He whispered so quietly. "Around fifty military men are guarding Ronald. He and the two other remaining Council Members are in there with five men I recognize from The Community." He looked at Chrissy. "Your girls and mom are not in there."

"Let's stick to the plan even though we are outnumbered. We have secret weapons and can take them down. Chrissy, re-member that you and I are to focus only on the Council Members and to banish the evil spirits into the Stones." Joseph deter-mined. "That's the only way to ensure the girls are safe."

Chrissy shook her head in answer. Her voice was too shaky to speak at the moment, and she didn't want the others to know.

"Agreed," Diego said right before his body started shaking, and he fell to the ground. Chrissy watched in shock as his body changed into one that was twice his normal size, full of brown hair and fangs that were larger than her head.

Diego didn't look back as he rushed into the room. Chrissy looked at Sharon as she phased and ran after Diego. Amazingly, she felt a sense of comfort, knowing they were on her side.

George and Katarina followed Sharon, and Chrissy was about to follow them when Henry grabbed her arm, causing both Chrissy and Joseph to pause. Henry leaned down and kissed her soundly on the mouth and said, "I love you." before leading her into the room that she considered the room of death.

CHAPTER 59

Chrissy was surprised to see only two men fighting while everyone stood there and watched. Why is no one moving? Henry reached out for emotion and felt nothing from anyone but the two men fighting and something coming from the hole in the ground. He knew it didn't make sense. Why would no one be feeling anything? Especially right now. He could feel heartbeats, so he knew they were not dead.

The hole in the cave floor started putting off a red glow which seemed to make the cave walls vibrate. The stronger the glow became, the more the room vibrated.

All the while, the two men fought. He recognized one of the men as Ronald Burgess, but he wasn't sure who the other one was. Whomever he was, Henry hoped he won the fight.

Henry thought the ceiling would cave in on them if the vibration didn't stop soon. The man Ronald was fighting turned, and Henry knew it was one of the other Council Members. Good. It looked like they were turning on one another.

What have we walked in on? Chrissy felt fear trickle through her entire body, but she pushed it down, trying hard to fight the rising panic. She could not allow fear to cause her to mess up. She looked at the scene in front of her, then at Henry and Joseph. They were also staring at the scene. Almost mesmerized.

Chrissy thought about that kiss and "I love you" she had

gotten from Henry, and warmth filled her.

Joseph thought about what his ancestors went through. He was thankful for the vision that had prepared him for this moment. He pulled on their strength and wisdom to guide him. He would not fail. When he looked at Chrissy, he saw his son. His blood. He would not allow these evil spirits to take her away from him.

Everyone who had come in the room before was standing as still as statues. Not even moving an inch.

We are too late. Henry felt the dread of being too late hit him. He wasn't scared to die, but he was scared to lose Chrissy and his mother. Not to mention the other people who had some-how wiggled their way into his heart.

Henry walked up to George and touched his hand, noth-ing. All he could do was move his eyes. "Move your eyes to the left if you saw where Katarina went."

"Now, Henry. You know it will take more than this to do me in." Katarina said from the swirl of smoke that circled Henry's legs.

Katarina then appeared in between Joseph and Chrissy, causing Chrissy to almost jump out of her skin. Katarina grabbed Chrissy's hand. "It's just me, Chris."

She kept ahold of Chrissy's hand and looked at Henry and Joseph. "I don't know how, but they have completed the sacrifice, and the spirit is escaping its prison. We must stick to the plan even without the help of the others."

Before they could move, a heavy mist started pouring out of the hole and into the room with them.

Ronald looked over at the mist escaping its prison and was glad. It gave him the needed zeal to finish the fight with the trai-tor. He had been shocked when Robert had tried to stab him but was prepared to defend himself. He was always on guard, ready for someone to try to overtake him.

Ronald took the knife away from Robert and stabbed him

dead in the heart, locking eyes with him as first the shock appeared on his face mere seconds before the life left his eyes and he dropped to the ground.

Chrissy knew she had no time to lose. Even though she felt raw terror tingling from the bottom of her feet and going all the way up to the hairs on her head, she had to push through. For her girls. For her mom. For Henry and the rest of the team.

She saw Ronald kill the other Council Member and knew the evil spirit living inside him would try to escape. She pulled out a Stone and walked towards the fallen Council Member as she started the chant:

i-ki-shi-ke wa-na-xe di-e e-ti da ko-zhi hi ni-ka-shi-ka de-do ki-we i^n-ch^{h}o^n

i-ki-shi-ke wa-na-xe di-e e-ti da ko-zhi hi ni-ka-shi-ka de-do ki-we i^n-ch^{h}o^n

Joseph took her other hand and joined in the chant with her. The evil spirit was not strong enough to fight them both, and within seconds, it was safely banished into the Stone.

Chrissy laughed with relief. They had done it! They had banished one evil spirit, and she felt energy racing through her. They could finish it. Together.

Henry was so proud, and he could feel the same emotion coming from Joseph. But, unfortunately, they didn't have time for a celebration. They had more evil spirits to take care of.

Ronald looked at the four of them like they were bothersome flies. He would have to take them out now before they caused some real damage.

They braced themselves for the fight. Chrissy and Joseph each had a Stone raised high, ready to start their chant. Henry and Katarina were poised to protect them from bodily harm.

Then something unexpected happened. The Mist surrounded Ronald, and within seconds he started gasping for air.

"What are you doing?" Finally, he croaked out, "I'm on your side!"

Finally, the mist left him, and he fell to the ground, holding his throat.

Chrissy watched the scene unfold with what she thought of as a weird fascination. She couldn't figure out why the thing that came out of the ground would attack one of its own subjects.

The mist floated around the room and stopped in front of Chrissy for a few seconds before it started changing forms. It was moving back towards Ronald and was becoming more and more human-like the closer it got to him.

Ronald jumped up and started heading in the other direction. He seemed desperate to get away from the mist turned human until he looked back at it and stopped dead in his tracks.

He stopped and looked intently at the human form of the spirit that had been released from its prison. Even in the dim cave, Chrissy could see he had turned white as a ghost.

Ronald couldn't believe his eyes. He watched as a bug crawled out of his daughter's eye and down her face before falling to the floor, and then he found his voice. "Barbara Jean?"

The human form of the spirit smiled a perfectly evil smile. "Hello, Daddy. Miss me?"

CHAPTER 60

I t walked to Ronald with its arms outstretched, and he felt a sense of relief and joy mixed together. His daughter was alive!

"How is this possible?" Ronald stared at Barbara Jean with unbelief on his face before walking to her.

Ronald opened his arms for the hug, but it never came. Instead, Barbara Jean picked up Robert's knife right as Ronald reached her and stabbed him in the gut. "That is for my mother."

Ronald looked down at his bleeding stomach in shock and confusion. "What? Why?" He felt his legs give out as he fell to the floor of the cave.

Barbara Jean leaned down and smiled. "Oh, Daddy. You had it coming. It doesn't feel good, does it? To have someone you thought loved you hurt you. To have them put you last in their life! You have no idea what I went through! To be thrown down a huge hole by my own father! The fear I felt as I was going down into the dark! Luckily for me, I slammed into the side on the way down, and I held on for dear life!"

Ronald held on to his bleeding stomach. "How did you know about me being your father? The spell I cast should have kept that information from you!"

"Oh, Daddy, to be so smart, you really do show signs of stupidity. Matthew gave me back my memories after we fell in love. He told me you promised not to sacrifice me!"

"I didn't have a choice! You have to believe me, Barbara Jean!"

Barbara Jean held the knife to Ronald's throat. "I was the only one who ever survived the fall. The Ancient One took it as a sign of my strength and took me as a temporary host! They turned me into one of them! I had to live knowing it was my own father who had decided to sacrifice my life to demons! To evil spirits who live below! The Ancient One tested me and, after finding me worthy, melded with me. I am no longer just Barbara Jean. I am also the Ancient One you sacrifice to!"

Even Chrissy could hear the raw panic in Ronald's voice. "Barbara Jean, please. Don't do this. We can rule together as Father and Daughter. I love you. I always have loved you and have regretted everything!"

"LIAR!!!" Barbara Jean screamed at Ronald with a fury like he had never known. She looked at him and stabbed him three more times, and at that moment, Ronald knew he was going to die. "I know EVERYTHING about your life! I know about all the sacrifices! MY MOTHER!!! MY HUSBAND!!! MATTHEW WAS THE ONLY MAN WHO EVER LOVED ME!!!"

Barbara Jean's face suddenly changed to one of peace. She smiled at Ronald like he was her best friend. "I know you don't love anyone but yourself. And that woman Jocelyn. Yeah, I know you love her. I've listened to you go on and on about her for years now. But don't you worry about her. I will be taking care of her real soon. She will also taste death at the end of my blade before this night is over."

"NOOOOOO!!!" All Chrissy heard was that thing planned to kill her mother, and she lost her mind.

She held up the Stone and started the chant to banish the woman/demon or whatever it was. All she knew was that Ronald was calling it Barbara Jean, but it couldn't be her grandmother. No way.

Chrissy didn't make it far. Barbara Jean looked at Chrissy with indifference, then she waved her hand and released all the military men from the enchantment.

"They had death in their eyes. And every single one of them had Chrissy in their sights."

Henry was right behind Chrissy, and he braced for the attack. He felt the adrenaline course through his veins before he attacked the men who came at Chrissy. He was outnumbered, but he fought with all he had to keep the men back so Chrissy and Joseph could banish the spirits.

Henry looked over at his mother just in time to see her run towards the threat, vanishing in a cloud of smoke.

Katarina knew she had to act quickly, or Chrissy would be dead. She surrounded the man with the bow and arrow trained on Chrissy and squeezed hard until he dropped the bow to the ground. Not satisfied, she enveloped his body until she felt his larynx crush, and he dropped to the ground beside his bow.

Henry watched his mother kill the man and wondered how she did it. He could only move around when he was in his other form. Not her; she could do almost anything she wanted in either state.

Another man ran at him, and he hit him square in the chest, sending him flying across the room.

Joseph and Chrissy stood hand in hand, Stones held high, chanting over and over. They had successfully banished one spirit from out of Ronald before the room erupted in nothing but chaos.

All the "wedding goers" had heard the commotion and poured in from the other room. After they saw Ronald bleeding on the ground, they thought Chrissy and Joseph were responsible, and they were screaming and crying for them to stop. Most all of them joined the military men in attacking Henry and trying to reach Chrissy and Joseph.

Lucas, Geoffrey, and Rose had made their way inside and

joined in the fight, trying to keep people away from Chrissy and Joseph.

Chrissy hated to see Rose mixed up in the fighting but was happy to see Rose holding her own. She and Geoffrey were tag-teaming people.

At that moment, Ronald met Chrissy's eyes, and she saw a sense of sadness there she had not expected. "Save your mother and girls. They are with her. Please. Ask Jocelyn to forgive me." He then looked at the people in the cave and said something Chrissy couldn't understand, and she stumbled backward when she heard growls permeate the entire cave.

She looked back and saw that Ronald must have somehow broken the spell Barbara Jean had cast. As a result, her crew was free and had joined in the fight!

Joseph repeated the chant while he held the stone high, beckoning the spirit to leave Ronald.

Chrissy was about to join Joseph when she saw Diego clamp down on someone's neck, ripping his head off his shoulders and spitting it on the ground. Chrissy was almost mesmerized as she watched the fight.

Henry was so fast. He sliced two throats before Chrissy could even blink. Katarina and George were doing the same.

Chrissy looked back at Ronald as he lay bleeding out, and she saw his eyes glaze over in near death.

Henry ran over to her and Joseph. "One spirit left Ronald already, and there is another one leaving him now! He must have had at least two of them inside him!"

Chrissy turned and started the chant with Joseph when, out of nowhere, Anthony Hightower let out a battle cry and ran towards Chrissy. He picked her up and headed to the hole where they dropped their sacrifices.

Henry had three men on him when he saw Chrissy get picked up, and he lost his mind. He usually didn't use his fangs to fight because things could get messy and he could lose control, but he made an exception. He was starting to tear the men to pieces so he could quickly get to Chrissy when George beat him to it.

George grabbed Anthony by the hair and jerked his head back, causing the man to scream out in pain before he released Chrissy from his grasp.

Chrissy grasped at the air as she started falling to the ground, hitting with a hard thump. Before she could get up, a woman came from behind her and pushed her down into the hole.

Henry heard Chrissy's scream as she went down, and he wasted no time diving into the hole behind her.

CHAPTER 61

Katarina looked at Joseph and saw the pain she felt reflected on his face. They both ran to the hole and looked down.

Joseph couldn't see that far, but Katarina let out a yelp of joy when she saw Chrissy and Henry sitting in the cage that the men had normally used to lower sacrifices down the hole.

"Crank the motor and get us out of here, Mom!"

He didn't have to ask her twice, and within seconds they were pulling them out of the cage and back on solid ground.

They looked around and saw only a handful of people were still alive. Diego and Sharon had tied them up, and they were lined against the wall. Some looked mad, while others looked apprehensive. Chrissy wondered what they would do with them.

The woman who had pushed Chrissy down the hole lay on the ground with a gash in her skull. *Ouch*, Chrissy thought.

The last Council Member was also dead. His body looked like it had been twisted into a pretzel. *How in the world?* Chrissy thought but decided she wouldn't even ask.

Joseph looked at Chrissy. "I was able to banish the spirit living in the one who now looks like a pretzel, thanks to Katarina. That makes four total we have successfully banished so far. But Chrissy, the other two are no longer here. We must find them and banish them and also the one called Barbara Jean."

"Where is she?" Chrissy looked everywhere in the cave, and Barbara Jean was nowhere to be found.

"She must have slipped out while we were fighting," Katarina said.

"We have to find her. She is going to go after my mother and kill her. Ronald used his dying breath to tell me my girls are with her. Where is Ronald's body?"

"It may have been taken. A few of them got away with some of the bodies."

Sharon had phased back into her human form, and she was ready to help. "Chrissy. I have been living in the Community for the past couple of weeks. I know where your girls are."

Lucas walked up to the group. His arm looked broken, and he was bleeding profusely from his head. "I will come help."

In the end, they decided that Henry, Diego, Sharon, and Lucas would go with Chrissy to find her girls while the rest stayed behind in the cave with Joseph to make sure the evil spirits didn't try to return.

They had been walking through the woods for what seemed like thirty minutes. "Sharon, I don't think this is the right way," Chrissy said. "We have been this way and haven't noticed any houses, much less a whole community."

"I may not remember where it is located, but I know it will be well hidden, and Sharon, you more than likely won't remember either," Lucas said in answer.

Sharon looked at Lucas like she wanted to kill him. And she did want to kill him but would wait for another time. "I watched every move you made after you brought me here. You only thought I was knocked out."

Diego itched to break Lucas's neck for what he had done to

his wife. "This isn't the same person, Diego. Joseph banished the spirit from Lucas, and he is different." Henry pointed out.

Diego reluctantly nodded.

Then Sharon stopped in front of a huge tree. "Right this way." She said as she walked right into the tree and disappeared.

Now I've seen it all. Henry thought. He looked at Chrissy and grabbed her hand as they both walked into the tree, with Diego and Lucas right behind them.

To their surprise, there was an entire community on the other side. "Wow. This is not what I expected. How far is it to Jocelyn's house?" Chrissy asked Sharon.

"Five minutes max."

Sure enough, they stopped outside a large, two-story home within five minutes. "Sharon, Chrissy, will you two stay out here while we go check it out?"

"Not a chance. My girls are in that house."

"Understood. Let's all go in but please, everyone, be quiet as a mouse. I need to listen for sounds and see if I can feel any emotions that shouldn't be there."

Henry eased into the front door and listened for noises. Nothing out of the ordinary. He could hear three people sleeping soundly. It had to be Jocelyn and the girls.

He put his finger to his mouth and whispered. "I can only sense three people here. Chrissy, you and I will go upstairs. Everyone else, please keep watch down here."

Chrissy opened the first door, and there on the bed curled up asleep were her babies. She had never been happier in her life than at that instant.

CHAPTER 62

Jocelyn was alarmed when she heard footsteps coming up the stairs. She had heard that Ronald was planning a surprise wedding for that night, but that would have been hours ago. She had been disappointed when no one had ever shown up to pick her and the girls up.

She eased the gun out of her side table and quietly opened her bedroom door. She saw a man standing in the hallway and felt her heart drop.

Henry felt fear. He turned and saw a woman standing with a gun pointed at his chest. "What are you doing here?"

Chrissy heard her mother's voice. "Mama!"

Henry could feel the confusion Jocelyn was experiencing. "Who said that?"

Chrissy walked out of the room, and Jocelyn pointed the gun at her then back at Henry. "Explain yourselves."

"You don't know who I am?" The exhaustion and sorrow coming from Chrissy were hitting Henry like a ton of bricks.

Jocelyn looked confused. "Should I know you? You do look a little familiar. Do you work in town? That doesn't explain why you are in my home uninvited."

Lucas walked up the stairs. "Jocelyn. There's been a terrible ordeal that has taken place tonight, and we need your help."

Jocelyn lowered the gun. "What's happened?"

Lucas walked up to her and put a rag to her face, and she immediately fell into his arms. "It's only chloroform. Ronald keeps it on hand for emergencies. We need to get her out of here now, and I knew she would put up a fight, so I borrowed some from Ronald's stash."

Chrissy shut her mouth that was open, ready to jump down Lucas's throat. "Henry, will you help me get the girls?"

Within minutes they had both girls and Jocelyn down the stairs. Diego ended up carrying Jocelyn since Lucas was struggling with his weight due to his injuries.

Chrissy smiled at Henry and mouthed thank you as they walked out of The Community and towards Henry's Jeep.

Barbara Jean melted into the shadows and kept her emotions turned off as she watched the group walk out of The Community.

She waited until they were long gone before she allowed the anger to settle in her stomach. She watched as the one they called Diego carried Jocelyn, and she dreamed of ripping her to pieces but would not do it if Chrissy were around.

Back at the cave, she needed to get away and knew everyone would worry more about protecting Chrissy than capturing her, so she made the military men go after Chrissy. No one knew they were under orders not to kill Chrissy.

Chrissy had been through a lot in her lifetime, and Barbara Jean decided she would not add more grief to her. At least not right now. She was surprised when she realized she felt something close to love for the woman Chrissy. She knew her son, Allen, had raised Chrissy as his daughter, and she felt a connection to Allen when she looked at Chrissy.

That was what she desired. A connection. To feel loved. She cast another look as they got farther away. Her revenge could wait. She would allow Chrissy some time with her mother before bringing her wrath down on the woman who had done what she hadn't been able to. Make Ronald Burgess love her.

"See you soon, Jocelyn." Barbara Jean whispered to the night before getting in Ronald's black Mercedes and driving out of Moon Lake, Arkansas.

EPILOGUE

"**H**appy Birthday to you, Happy Birthday to you…dear Jessica, Happy Birthday to youuuuuu!!!" The group of people sang in almost harmony to six-year-old Jessica as she blew out the candles on top of her Scooby Doo cake.

Jessica and Lela giggled at the way Henry got loud and silly when he sang Happy Birthday. Chrissy watched as Jessica leaned over and kissed Henry on the cheek, and her heart fluttered with happiness.

It had been a little over three months since that horrific night at the cave, and a lot had changed since then. Chrissy thought back to everything that had happened, and her mind was almost blown. Again.

Every now and then, she would pinch herself to make sure it was real. To make sure she wasn't in an episode of The Twilight Zone.

Chrissy and the girls had moved into The Lodge and re-opened it with the help of Geoffrey and Rose. There wasn't an awful lot of guests right now, but Chrissy had a plan in mind to bring business in.

Katarina and Joseph had both opted to stay on at The Lodge. They agreed they needed to be around, so the team had backup when the spirits showed back up.

Katarina and Henry were in talks about opening up an

Agency near Moon Lake. After everything they had all been through, they were thinking about expanding it to handle more than just Vampirism.

Joseph had been busy trying to figure out how to make more arrowhead necklaces. If everyone on the team had one, it would be easier to locate the spirits. He knew they had not gone far. They were just laying low, biding their time and lurking in the shadows.

George decided to travel the world. Katarina had shown him all the ways to hunt animals and which human foods were easiest to digest. He had promised to return within a year or so.

Diego and Sharon had moved closer to Moon Lake to continue looking for her sister, Brenda. Sharon had come clean to Diego and asked for forgiveness. He had forgiven her as long as she made a promise to never keep things from him again.

Jocelyn also took a room at The Lodge, but Chrissy could see a sadness in her that was even greater than when they lost her dad, Allen Kensington. She had embraced the girls with open arms, and Chrissy was thankful for that.

However, she had not been so willing to embrace Chrissy. At least not yet. She had a wariness in her eyes when she looked at Chrissy that made Chrissy sad. But she was simply happy to have her mama alive and with them. Plus, she was determined to change that look back to the one of love she had grown up with. They had always been close, and Chrissy would try to get that back.

Lucas was still the Sheriff, and he had helped the people who survived the horrific night settle back into The Community. They had all agreed that was best for now until they could figure out how to lift the spell they were under.

"Thank you, Grandma!!!" Jessica exclaimed when she opened a present wrapped in pink with a cute little toy pony inside. "I've always wanted one of these!"

Chrissy smiled at Anne as they watched Frank pick Jessica

up and swing her around, "That was your last present. You ready for some cake?"

"Yes!!!"

Anne already had Lela on her lap, and she held her hands out for Jessica to join them. "Come here, and I will help you cut the first piece."

A couple of hours later, Chrissy. She sat on the bench overlooking Moon Lake, admiring the water and how the moon's reflection made the water glisten.

She heard footsteps coming up behind her and smiled. She almost felt like a schoolgirl again. Henry had told her he loved her, and then he showed it. Not many men, immortal or not, would jump in a hole that could lead to imminent death for a woman. But Henry did without hesitation. She had already developed feelings for him, but after that, it was extra hard not to fall head over heels. She had stopped even trying to fight it.

"Hi, Henry."

Henry could hear the smile in her voice, and he was elated. He was elated at how someone like him could ever be so fortunate to have a chance with someone like her.

They both knew they were not out of the woods yet. They had two more spirits to get rid of in the future. But not this night. This night was for peace. This night was for happiness.

Chrissy held out her hand, and he took it and kissed it before sitting by her on the bench. He looked at Moon Lake and did something he hadn't done since he was a human. He planned for a future of happiness in Moon Lake. With Chrissy and the girls.

Chrissy squeezed his hand and laid her head on his shoulder. He leaned down and kissed the top of her head before she turned, and he kissed her lips. He could feel Chrissy's butterflies in her stomach at his kiss and was not surprised when he realized his own set of butterflies were in his stomach, and they matched hers.

Henry was thankful for Destin, Florida, and for his love of

deep-sea fishing that led him to his friend James Kensington. But most of all, he was grateful for how his friendship with James had brought Henry to Moon Lake and happiness.

the end

ACKNOWLEDGEMENT

I would like to thank my husband, Mark Brewer, for supporting my writing even though I probably paid more attention to what was happening with Chrissy and Henry than him these past few months. My daughter, Cassidy Snyder, for reading my chapters and giving me advice on things that needed to be added or updated. For my daughter, Carissa Brewer and son-in-law, Logan Snyder, for listening to my nonstop rambling about my book. My sister-in-law, Brandi Hudson, for reading my rough draft and encouraging me. Last but not least, Stacy Williams, for reading the finished product, giving me advice, then rereading the new finished product and giving me more advice - for truly helping me see things through a reader's eyes.

Y'all rock!

ABOUT THE AUTHOR

Leah writes supernatural books, is a blogger, Bible class teacher, and has worked at the same Telecommunications company for almost twenty-five years. She is a wife and mother who loves being able to spend time with her family.

Leah was born and raised a small town girl in the beautiful, natural state of Arkansas. She loves Arkansas, but her heart is at the beach. She dreams of living in a small, coastal town someday.

Find Leah Brewer online at:
www.LeahBrewerAuthor.com

TO MY READERS

Dear Reader,

    I hope you enjoyed reading the first book in our series about Moon Lake and the people living there. These characters have a place in my heart and I have loved writing their first story!

    I am currently working on our second book and will update my website with publishing dates soon.

    Please feel free to send me feedback at leahbrewerauthor-@outlook.com or at leahbrewerauthor.com. I welcome it as I am growing as a new author!

    If you have a few minutes, please leave me a review on Amazon. I would truly appreciate it. :)

Bless you,

Leah

Made in the USA
Columbia, SC
03 June 2021